Little Sister

Kara Dalkey

Little Sister

JANE YOLEN BOOKS / HARCOURT BRACE & COMPANY

SAN DIEGO / NEW YORK / LONDON

Library of Congress Cataloging-in-Publication Data
Dalkey, Kara, 1953–
Little sister/Kara Dalkey.—1st ed.
p.   cm.
"Jane Yolen Books."
Summary: Thirteen-year-old Fujiwara no Mitsuko, daughter of
a noble family in the imperial court of twelfth-century Japan,
enlists the help of a shape-shifter and other figures from Japanese
mythology in her efforts to save her older sister's life.
ISBN 0-15-201392-x
[1. Supernatural—Fiction.   2. Sisters—Fiction.   3. Japan—
History—Heian period, 794–1185—Fiction.]   I. Title.
PZ7.D1565Li   1996
[Fic]—dc20   96-2556

Text set in Electra
Designed by Camilla Filancia

First edition
F E D C B A

To BARRY *and* SANDI

from their own

little sister

Little Sister

My name is Fujiwara no Mitsuko
and I am the little sister of Amaiko.
Goranu, who reads this over my
shoulder as I write, says this
is unworthy—that I am much more.
But this is how I have seen myself,
esteemed reader, for so much of
my life and especially in the
troubled times just past. Perhaps
once you have read my story, you
and Goranu, too, will understand.

Little Sister of Earth

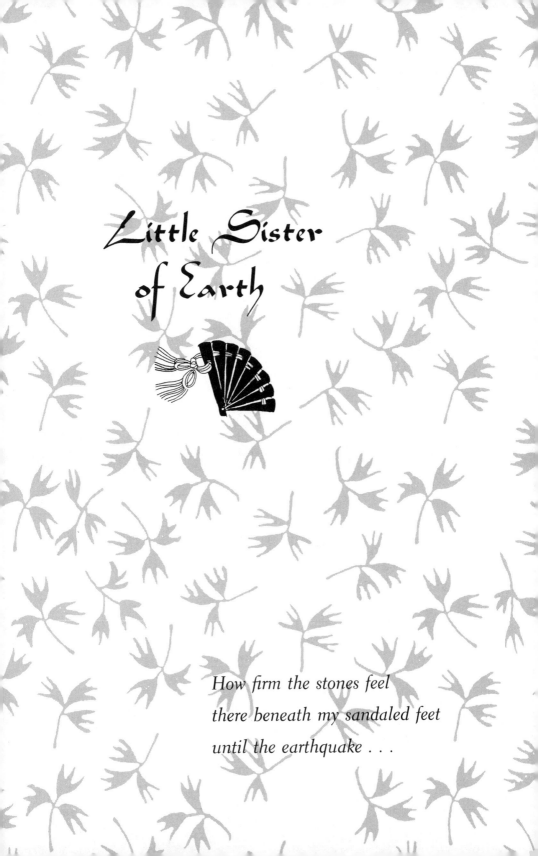

How firm the stones feel
there beneath my sandaled feet
until the earthquake . . .

I WILL BEGIN my story in the ninth year of the reign of Emperor Shirakawa. I was born thirteen years before, but those years are inconsequential, so I will not— Do not strike me with your feathered fan, Goranu! You know perfectly well why I write it down this way. If you please, go and let me work in peace.

So. It was at the Turning of the Year that the Masters of Yin-Yang in the Divination Bureau informed Papa that it would be an eventful year for our family. Truly they had cast their divinations well, for so it came to be.

On the fifth day of the First Month, Papa received a high
administrative post at the Imperial Bestowing of Ranks, allow-
ing him to at last wear the black robes of office. On the tenth
day of that month, my little brother, Yūshō, had his First
Trousers ceremony and a cousin of the Emperor himself tied
Yūshō's sash.

In the Second Month, Mama finished her monotogari
and all the Court read it—they said her writing promised to
surpass that of Lady Murasaki someday. Because of Papa's
new rank, there were whispers my older sisters Kiwako and
Sōtōko, who were both fifteen, might be called to serve at
the Imperial Palace.

And in the Third Month, as the first cherry blossoms appeared on the trees, my oldest sister, Amaiko, met the man
she was to marry.

I must stop and explain something (how I wish I had
Mama's skill at this!). Of all my sisters, and my little brother,
too, I am most especially fond of Amaiko. Her hair is the
black of the purest inkstone, and her features like the delicate
brushstrokes of the best artists. Her skill with poetry was the
talk of the court, and she played the koto so well that nobles
and ministers would find reasons to visit our house just to
hear her play.

On cool evenings, she and I would sit on the veranda and
watch the moon. She would teach me some fingerings upon
the koto, and I would gaze upon her and wish that someday
I could be like her. But though I felt like a toad gazing upon
a crane, my envy was never bitter. I was content that fate
permitted me just to be in her presence, to hear her laugh

and chide me with a smile; to watch her hands move like leaves floating on the Kamo River.

Forgive me. I must pause, before my sleeves become as damp with tears as they were with the dew of those spring evenings.

There. It happened at the Winding Water Banquet on the Festival of the Snake. Our family was invited by our more illustrious relatives to attend the banquet at the Imperial Palace. Our cousins had sent us new silk gowns to wear, and we were all very excited. Mama asked us if we wanted to display our dolls this year, but we flounced around in our new finery and said, "No, we are too old for dolls now. We are going to climb the heights and touch the clouds of Heaven."

Mama shook her head, smiling. "Take care, my no-longer-children, for dragons live on the heights, and the rains of Heaven may wash you away."

We laughed, of course.

The banquet was so exciting I thought I would faint. Special platforms for the Ladies had been set up in the Cherry Tree Garden, surrounded by curtains of blue silk painted with water designs in which the shapes of snakes were cunningly hidden. All of the Court Ladies artfully let their sleeves drape out beneath the curtains, to display their fashionable taste. I had never seen such beautiful gowns or such well-kept manners. I felt very much a goat among deer—yet I was so happy, I did not care. There was such pleasant conversation, and now and then one of the Court Ladies would place a poem on a wooden boat and float it on the stream that ran beside our platform. We all received love poems; even I got one! It read:

> *Is this a doll come to life?*
> *Such perfection surely cannot be real —*
> *or is it but a dream?*

Not a very good poem, but I had to answer. I confess my hand shook as I wrote on a piece of pale pink paper:

> *Too old for dolls,*
> *too young for the serpent stream,*
> *I sit and admire —*
> *but dare not let my sleeves get wet!*
> *You'd best continue dreaming.*

Yes, it was too long and clumsy, but I had not had much practice at such things. My admirer must have thought it clever, though, for he sent back this reply:

> *The pine tree*
> *beside the serpent stream*
> *will dream, dew drenched,*
> *until another Spring.*

There was a black feather with the poem, though I could not have imagined why.

My sisters Kiwako and Sōtoko sat and giggled over the poems they received, but they would not show them to me, nor the replies they wrote. Their poems were probably stupid ones, anyway. Amaiko got the most poems sent to her, for she was already known by the Court. One of the poems she received was:

Ah! A new cherry blossom
arrives to grace our tree!
Though she blooms late among so many,
still is her beauty treasured,
for it prolongs our Spring.

Amaiko was showered with so many poems that she waved her hands in bewilderment, scattering the paper like flower petals on the wind.

"How can I respond to them all?" she said with delighted frustration.

"Let us help," said the Court Ladies. And they divided up the poems amongst each other, seeming to enjoy replying to Amaiko's as much as they would their own. One such reply was:

Take care, lest the welcoming wind
blows too much dust upon our new blossom.
She might fall from the tree!

Amaiko looked at me and said, "Here, Mitsuko, you must answer one. You are good at poems."

I was so pleased that she would ask me that I blushed and hid my face behind my sleeves. I picked up the nearest paper. It had been folded into the shape of a plum blossom, and I carefully unfolded it. The poem within read:

The whispering leaves
bring the fragrance of a new flower.
Though I have caught but little of her scent,
like the mountain wisteria,
it fills my heart with longing.

I scarcely knew what to say. For all I knew, I could be replying to the Emperor himself (though I would expect the Son of Heaven to be a better poet). Finally I wrote:

> *This small spring puddle*
> *holds but a reflection of the new flower*
> *yet sees her basking in the warm mountain wind.*

There, I thought, *that should be harmless enough.* I sent it back with a little mirror I begged off one of the Court Ladies.

After a time, we heard laughter from the men's pavilion, and many of the lines quoted from the replies we sent. I thought I heard mine read, followed by loud hoots and exclamations. Ashamed, I buried my face in my sleeves.

Before long, a poem came back:

> *O fortunate puddle!*
> *Would I could hold the flower's image*
> *as close as you do.*
> *Pray reflect my warmth to her,*
> *that she might turn in my direction.*

It was followed by others even more impertinent, such as the one in which the poet wished to cool his wandering feet in the puddle's mud.

I wanted to crawl away in embarrassment. But Amaiko and the Court Ladies were very kind. "The men have had too much sake and are only good for foolishness now," they said. "Do not take it to heart."

Soon it grew dark and cooler, and we retreated to an inner pavilion for the banquet. Mama had told me that a true lady will eat as little as possible in public, but there were so many new and interesting dishes that I confess I ate a great deal.

"Look, the puddle is filling rapidly," said an older Court Lady.

"Perhaps she prefers not to dry up," said another, pointedly, to the first.

"She is grateful for receiving the gift of the clouds of Heaven," said Amaiko, gently, "and wishes not to seem rude by spurning it."

I thought of some replies, but my mouth was full. I will never make a suitable Court Lady, I fear.

But forgive me. I am writing too much about myself, and I wanted to tell about Amaiko. That night, Kiwako and Sōtōko and I shared a room; Amaiko had one beside us. We were all very tired, yet still so excited it was hard to sleep. We heard a man's voice speak softly outside Amaiko's shōji, and Kiwako and Sōtōko started to giggle.

"Stop it," I said. "Isn't it natural that she should receive attention if she wants?"

"Ah, but will she be a rabbit or a crab?" asked Sōtōko.

"She will keep us up all night if she is hard shelled like the crab," said Kiwako. "So let us hope she is a rabbit and gives in swiftly."

"No, no," giggled Sōtōko. "If she is a rabbit, she will be noisier and still keep us awake."

"Stop it!" I hissed.

"Don't be jealous, Little Puddle," said Kiwako. "Maybe your wandering poet will come to drown himself in you."

They dissolved into peals of giggles, and I rolled away from them in shame and despair. I only hoped Amaiko did not hear us.

The following morning, I awoke just as the gray light of dawn was filling the room. Kiwako and Sōtōko were still asleep. I heard a noise out on the veranda and I crept to the sliding door. Silently, I opened it — just a crack — and peered outside.

Amaiko knelt at the edge of the veranda. Her long, loose raven hair flowed like a thick brushstroke down her back. Her oyster-colored robe blended into the morning mist, as if she were part of it, or a spirit partially departed.

A young man stood in the garden at the edge of the veranda, holding her hand. He was handsome, and his bright green-and-yellow jacket stood out from the mist as though defying its attempts to mute and absorb him. As he gazed at my sister, I could tell he loved her very much. As they softly said their parting words, I wished I could hear them. Yet I was glad, in a way, that those whispers remained secret.

The young man looked at the lightening sky, then he bowed to Amaiko. He turned and strode away through the garden, daring the weeds to leave dew on his cloak. My sister watched him until he climbed into his carriage and could be seen no more. She hid her face within her sleeves.

I wanted to call out to her, but I did not. I could not disturb such a perfect moment. Amaiko silently returned to her room and I closed the shōji, my heart filled with the beauty of what I had seen.

———

The memory is even more poignant now that I know their fates.

But forgive me. I should not leap ahead of my story.

We soon learned the young gentleman's name — Koga no Yugiri. His next-morning poem arrived just after his departure. He must have written it in his carriage. To my surprise, Mama already had a bottle of plum wine and silk robes to give to the servant who brought the poem. I wished I could have read it or Amaiko's reply, but when I asked her about them, she only smiled and shook her head.

The next night, I had to keep Sōtōko and Kiwako from spying on Amaiko and her new companion. I wondered if our tussling and hair pulling might have disturbed the lovers, but the next morning, Amaiko showed no sign of anger.

By now it was clear that Yugiri did not want merely a moonlit liaison (as so often is the style at Court), but he actually wanted to marry Amaiko! Again I fought with my sisters over who should take the official three rice cakes and Papa's letter of acceptance into Amaiko's room. Mama became quite exasperated with us and finally chose our little brother, Yūshō, as the messenger. I was so upset, I cried myself to sleep that night.

The following week, we had a big feast, and finally we all got a close look at our new brother-in-law.

"How handsome he is!" said Kiwako.

"She is so lucky," grumbled Sōtōko.

"She deserves no less," I said.

"Is she his main wife, or does he have one already?" asked Kiwako.

"Mama said he had a wife before who died having a baby.

So Amaiko will be his main wife, if not his first," said Sōtōko.

"Well, that's better, isn't it?" I said. "A first wife gets a child for a husband."

They looked at me as though I were possessed.

It happened that Yugiri was a distant relative of the Emperor and had excellent prospects of advancement, so it was no wonder Papa agreed to the match instantly. We all liked Yugiri because he was generous and kind; he brought presents of a short sword for Yūshō and lots of gowns and fans for my sisters and me. He would say to us, "Be careful! Now that I have seen your beauty, I will tell all my brothers and cousins and they will be clamoring for your attention." He made us laugh, and we could see why Amaiko loved him.

As Yugiri did not yet have his own manor, Amaiko stayed with us and he came and visited us often. It was beautiful to see them together on those warm spring evenings. He played the flute as she played the koto, and their music intertwined marvelously. I would stay awake late just to watch them watching the moon, so elegant was the scene they created, like a passage from the *Genji* monotogari. When Yugiri was not with Amaiko or joking with us, he would sit and talk politics with Papa. He brought such liveliness into our home—

Pardon me. A raindrop seems to have appeared on the paper. I wish it were not late Spring, so I would not have to see the cherry blossoms fall.

So the happy weeks passed, until the Seventh Month. One morning I awoke to a miserable damp heat and air that smelled of ashes. I wondered if there was a funeral nearby.

Papa and Yugiri seemed to hurry through the house with grim faces, and Mama hid herself in her room. None of the servants would answer questions, saying only, "There are things no lady should hear." I sat alone by the bamboo curtains of my room, determined, hopelessly, not to care.

The Seventh Month is called the Poem-Writing Month, but the only verses I could think of were dreary and distressing. It was so hot I didn't want to move. Though my kimonos were of the lightest silk, I felt like a steamed rice cake beneath them.

About midday, I heard a familiar whistle coming down the street beside our house. It was the bakery girl, Mochi, probably returning from a delivery to one of the noble houses, or perhaps the Palace itself. Nearly every day for the past year or so I had heard her go by; her whistle was reassuring. Unlike me, she was free to go about the city and see everything — nobody cares if a mere rice cake girl shows her face. I envied her, sometimes. Now and then, I would call her over and talk to her. Mama would have been scandalized if she knew I bothered to converse with such a lowly person. Had I been caught, I would simply have claimed that I was asking what wares the bakery had today; but I never was caught.

So on that hot morning, just as Mochi's whistle came past my curtain, I called out, "What is that bird who so loudly sings in the street?"

The whistling stopped. "What is that breeze that comes down from the mountain?"

I replied, "It is a summer wind brought low by the heavy air."

Mochi said, "It is a simple bird who flies everywhere."

"Ah, simple bird, pause awhile and tell me what you have seen."

"What can I have seen that a mountain cannot? Do clouds obscure your vision?"

"I think it is smoke, for I smell ashes on the wind."

"Ah. But what does a mountain care what happens at its feet?"

"Stop that." The heat made me impatient. "You know you can see things I do not. Everyone around here is acting strangely. I want to know what is going on."

There was a pause. "A bird cannot live on wind alone. I have work to do."

I slapped the straw mat beside me. "I will give you my third-best gown and my second-best fan if you will tell me."

"In that case —" And the girl actually hopped up on my veranda and sat just outside my curtain.

The nerve! I admired her temerity, but I desperately hoped no one would see her. Astonished, I said, "You are a bold bird!"

"The bird that comes to the master's hand can expect more reward. Give me my gifts and I will sing for you."

I made a noise like Papa when he is annoyed and I crawled to my clothing chest. I did not search within it but grabbed the first kimono and fan my hands touched. I suspected I may have been giving her my first-best fan and my fourth-best gown, but I did not care. I stuffed them under the bamboo curtain at her and said, "Sing!"

"Ah, most gladly, Puddle-on-the-Mountain."

"Do not call me that."

"A thousand apologies, my Lady. Well, the short of it is,

the monks from Mount Hiei and the Temple of Chizoku have come into the city."

"Are they performing services here?"

Mochi' laughed. "No, Lady. They have brought their sacred tree and sacred altar and they are roaming the city, setting fire to noblemen's houses."

I put my hand to my throat. Fire is the greatest fear; our houses burn so easily. "Why do they do this?"

"They say the city has fallen into wickedness. They have even marched up to the Palace gates and chastised the Emperor."

"No!"

"If you ask me, I think they just want to be paid to go away. But they seem very angry. Each temple claims that the Emperor favors the other one."

"How dare they? Surely the Emperor's guard will stop them?"

"And chance the bad luck brought by harming a priest?" ·

"But what will become of us?"

"Perhaps the mountain will stay out of the fire's way until the rains of Heaven put it out. Uh-oh. I see my brother coming. This bird had better fly. Good luck to you, my Lady!" And she was gone.

I could hardly eat or sleep for the next two days, so afraid was I. I dared not ask anyone about what the rice cake girl had said, for fear I would be asked how I knew.

On the third day following, I awoke in the darkness to the sound of feet running through the house. My shōji slid open and someone came in.

"Who is it?" I managed to say.

"Do not be afraid," said Neuchinashi, one of Papa's servants. "But you must get up and go to the front of the house right away!"

Someone else came in and I heard them pick up my kimono chest. I threw on the outer robes that lay beside me and hurried out. Everyone seemed to be running and whispering.

There was a touch on my shoulder and Mama said, "You must go to the gate. There are carriages waiting for us."

"But what is happening?" The smell of smoke was quite heavy in the air.

"No questions now. Just hurry!"

"Is Amaiko—"

"Go!"

I went, unsure as to whether I should veil my face since the sun had not yet risen. I could hardly see as I ran down the front walk to the gate.

Several ox-drawn carriages stood there, men loading them hastily, as though whipped by demons. I only watched a moment before I heard Amaiko whisper from the nearest carriage, "Mitsuko! Get in!"

I climbed clumsily through the back door of the carriage. Kiwako and Sōtōko were already inside, cowering together in one corner. Amaiko helped me sit on one of the large baskets against the carriage wall. The baskets were apparently stuffed with our belongings. "What is happening?" I asked.

"It is the end of the world," said Sōtōko, softly.

"Hush," said Amaiko. "It is true we are in danger, but Yugiri says we may escape to safety."

"Where are we going?" I asked.

"Papa owns a mountain lodge in Tamba Province," said Amaiko. "Yugiri is leading us there so that Papa will know we are safe until the danger in the city passes."

"Is our house on fire?"

"No. And with Amida's blessing we will be spared such a thing."

Just then, Mama breathlessly climbed into the carriage, helped by two servants. She sat quickly and closed the door.

"Is Papa coming with us?" asked Kiwako.

"No, he must stay in the city and help His Majesty. He may come join us later, or send for us to return when all is well."

"Have you ever been to this mountain lodge?" I asked Mama.

"No, but I have heard your father describe it often. You will like it, Mitsu-chan. It sounds like a beautiful place, with lots of waterfalls and rock gardens and views of the pines on the mountains."

Mama's eagerness to cheer me instead filled me with greater fear. I simply nodded. "Where is little Yūshō?"

"He rides up with Yugiri and the menservants. He refused to ride in the women's carriage."

Amaiko laughed. "So soon after his trousers are tied, and already he thinks them too short."

This made the rest of us smile. Outside, I heard the ox driver call, and there came the snap of a whip. The carriage lurched forward. Kiwako and Sōtōko moaned. I pulled my kimonos tighter around me and leaned against Mama. I had never been anywhere outside the city. In fact, I had never been away from home for more than three days at a time.

Amaiko put her hand on my shoulder. "Do not worry," she said, as if hearing my thoughts. "We will return soon."

I was shaking from too little sleep and too much care. I was glad the carriage shuddered as it rumbled down the street, for it disguised my trembling. I heard no other sound outside the carriage except the turning of the wheels and the plodding of the ox hooves. The morning birds seemed to have fled the city, too.

At last there were rays of sunlight coming through the bamboo canopy of the carriage. Mama was dozing on Amaiko's shoulder. I dared to lift the curtain on the window and peek at the world outside.

I could see Heian Kyō nestled in the hills just below us, and the hillsides were covered with summer flowers. The sight would have been beautiful but for the gray pall that hung over the city. I could see columns of smoke rising here and there, and I wondered if one of them was from our house.

"What do you see?" asked Kiwako.

"Nothing," I said, closing the curtain.

In a while, the carriage was moving more steeply uphill, and there were many turns in the road. The breeze blowing in through the window smelled less of smoke and more of pine and sweet flowers. I peeked again out the window. The sky was blue and the sun was very bright. Colorful birds, disturbed by our passing, flew up from the bushes beside the road.

Shortly we stopped to refresh ourselves. Mama brought out some covered bowls of dried fish and pickled vegetables.

It seemed odd and wonderful to have a meal in a carriage amid strange surroundings. The food tasted particularly good, almost as good as the cherries I once stole from a neighbor's tree.

After we ate and the carriages rolled forward again, Kiwako and Sōtōko began to sing a song they had heard at the Palace. The song was about oyster fishermen. It seemed silly to sing about the sea so high in the mountains — perhaps that's why they chose it. One by one, the rest of us joined in, and we were a jolly group indeed.

At about the tenth verse, we heard sound up ahead. Mama waved her hand to hush us.

I heard Yugiri, from a distance, say, "What do you want?"

The voice that followed was rough and I could not understand the words. Mama's eyes went very wide.

"Mama-chan, what—"

"Shush."

Yugiri said something more, about our being on imperial business, in a threatening growl.

In response there came a harsh laugh, and I heard movement all around us outside the carriages.

"Get in the baskets," Mama hissed.

"But—"

"Do as I say!" Her voice permitted no dissent. I had never seen her move so quickly. She shoved us out of the way and opened all of the large baskets we had been sitting on. "Get in, one to each, and do not move or speak until I tell you to."

Amaiko, seeming to understand what Mama was doing, helped Kiwako and Sōtōko and me into the baskets, stuffing all of our clothing down inside until no hem was hanging over the edges.

"You, too," I said as she was closing the lid on my basket.

Amaiko nodded and said, "As soon as the rest of you are safe." She closed the lid and I heard the bamboo latch slide into place just as someone rattled the back door of our carriage.

"Open up!" said a man, roughly.

I heard Mama say, "Who are you? How dare you? What do you want?" The door was wrenched open and Mama screamed.

I heard the rough voice say, "Oho! Look what I have found!"

Mama and Amaiko were pulled out of the carriage.

I bit my hand, thinking, *No, no, no! This cannot be happening!*

From up ahead of our carriage I heard the clash of swords and the screams of horses and men. I wrapped my arms tighter around myself and tried to recite the Lotus Sutra. Kiwako and Sōtōko keened and whimpered in the baskets beside me. I tried to remember the names of all my ancestors and invoke them as we do at the O-Bon Festival, begging them for help.

This is very hard to write. My heart even now is heavy as stone, though these events are long past. Yet it is part of the story and I must continue, painful as these words may be.

I do not remember how long I crouched there, trying not to hear the horror around me. It seemed a very long time. I remember that after the third recital of names, there was an eerie silence, broken only by distant weeping.

Unable to wait any longer, I managed to jiggle the latch of my basket loose, and I stumbled out.

"Mitsuko, be careful! Remember what Mama said!"

"I have to go see."

"Let us out, too!"

"In a minute." I jumped out of the open carriage door, not caring that my sleeve caught and tore on the rough bamboo. Outside, everything was still, as if the kamis of the air held their breath. I ran toward the front of the carriage and stopped.

Bodies of servants familiar to me, and strange men with shaved heads and gray robes, lay in disarray everywhere. Little Yūshō, holding his tiny short sword in front of him, wandered around in bewilderment. I saw the last of the oxcarts ahead of us disappear around a bend in the road. And to the side of the road, I saw Mama and Amaiko. My sister's kimonos were half torn away. But she did not seem to care — she was kneeling, staring at something that lay before her.

I ran up to Mama. She threw her arms around me.

"What has happened?" I said.

"Oh, Mitsu-chan," she said between sobs. "The warrior monks, they have robbed us."

"Where is Yugiri?"

Mama looked at the ground and did not reply. Over her shoulder, I saw two servants reverently bearing away something heavy in a bloodstained sheet of silk.

I stood and started to run to them but the servant Neuchinashi stopped me, tears streaming down his face. "No, Lady, you mustn't look. You must not touch the dead. It is not proper. It is too horrible."

I tore myself away from his babbling and buried my face in Mama's shoulder. We held each other, weeping, for a time.

When I could, I turned to Amaiko. I sighed, putting my arm around her. She did not move. She did not speak. She did not cry. She only stared, her face like a Noh mask, at Yugiri's bright, fallen tachi sword.

What followed seemed as if it were occurring in a dream. Servants appeared from out of the bushes or rose, wounded, from amongst those on the road. Strange men on horseback, wearing fur-trimmed armor, rode up and spoke to Mama. These men, Mama later told me, had come from the local daimyo, Lord Tsubushima. They had been sent to welcome us but arrived only in time to see us attacked by the warrior priests. Without their help, we would all have been killed. But as reward, the daimyo's men had demanded nearly half of what the thieves had left of our belongings.

Of those servants who remained, several volunteered to take the bodies of the slain back to Heian Kyō to be properly cremated.

"We should go back, too," I said.

Mama gathered herself together. "No. We must continue on. It is not yet safe for us to return."

Somehow, we got Amaiko back into our carriage, although she still would not speak or move of her own volition. Kiwako and Sōtōko were freed from their baskets, and our expressions told them all they feared was true. The servants gathered whatever could be salvaged from the plunder the fleeing monks and the rescuing warriors had left on the road, and we proceeded on to the mountain lodge in silence.

Little Sister of Ice

Behold the pinecone
entombed in the winter ice.
So, too, is my heart.

*W*E TRAVELED FOR another day and a half, until we reached the mountain lodge. That night we stayed in the carriage, stopped by the side of the road. It rained and water leaked through the bamboo roof onto us . . . as if our sleeves needed to be any damper. We ate little and spoke not at all. Mama watched Amaiko, who still showed no movement or interest in anything. Kiwako and Sōtōko held each other, now and then weeping. I sat huddled to myself, wondering how the world could so suddenly become wicked. We jumped every time the wind shook our frail shelter. We could hear the daimyo's men calling to one another, and as nothing further untoward happened that night, we eventually came to realize we were protected.

It continued to rain lightly the following day. We spent many hours sitting in the damp and dripping carriage and did not arrive at the lodge until evening. When the ox driver called out, "There it is!" all of us but Amaiko crowded around the window. But we could scarcely believe what we saw.

It was more dismal than I could have imagined, even in my sorrow. There was a building in view, but weeds choked what should have been gardens. The paper on the shōjis was stained and torn. The cloth on the bamboo blinds was frayed and rotting. Clearly no one had lived there for a very long time.

"By the merciful Amida," breathed Mama, "what has your father done to us? Did he know it would be like this?"

"It looks haunted," said Kiwako.

"Hush," said Sōtōko, glancing warily at Amaiko.

I thought it was only fitting, in a way. To have found a beautiful house would have made our sorrow seem out of place. What better reminder of the transience of joy, the illusion that is life, than a house deserted and decayed? I tried to form poems in my mind, but the ruined lodge was a poem in itself.

Mama, however, was incensed. As the carriage pulled as far as it could into the weed-covered courtyard, she jumped out, not minding the rain. "You!" I heard her say to the nearest horseman. Kiwako, Sōtōko, and I peered out to watch.

"What is it, Lady?"

"This cannot possibly be the proper place."

"This is your husband's lodge, Lady. There has been no mistake."

"Does your Lord, Tsubushima, know its condition?"

"Lady, we thought your lord had arranged for its care. Lord Tsubushima has been too busy to check on every dwelling in his province."

Mama fumed for a moment. "You cannot possibly expect us to stay here."

The horseman rubbed his chin. "Well, it is another day's journey, at least, to my Lord's castle. But I am sure you ladies would be most welcome there, as we almost never get visitors from the capital. Lord Tsubushima was delighted to hear we would have such courtly ladies nearby." The horseman smiled at us and we ducked our heads back into the carriage.

"Is that his horse or him that I smell?" said Kiwako.

"Did you see how squat and ugly he is? said Sōtoko.

"I don't like the way he looked at us," I said.

Amaiko just sat staring at the floor, as if she heard nothing.

"Nonsense," snapped Mama to the horseman. "We would not think of imposing upon your too-busy Lord. We will make the best of it here."

"As you wish, Lady. We soldiers must return tomorrow, however. Shall I take a message to Lord Tsubushima for you?"

"Tell him this:

> *Tears and raindrops*
> *steal the ink from my brush*
> *to write their own sad tale.*
>
> *I am left without words.*"

Then she added, "Have him send carpenters to us."

I admired how my mother could compose such a poem even in our poor situation. The horseman seemed to have admiration in his voice as well.

"I will tell him, Lady. Good luck to you and your family." He rode away, and Mama ordered the servants to unpack what was left of our household.

We managed to find one central room of the house with no leaks. It had a small stone hearth in the middle, in which we lit some coals. In the mountains it was much cooler than in Heian Kyō, so we had to huddle around the hearth, even though it was late summer. No one said much. We listened to the spatter of the rain on the roof and the hiss of the little fire. We ate the last of the seaweed-and-poppy-seed rice cakes that Mama had packed. They were damp and sticky and tasted of mold.

"What will become of us?" said Sōtōko, at last.

"Do not worry," said Mama. "By now your father knows what has happened. He will send help."

But I knew that no matter what help arrived, our lives had changed. The World Above the Clouds could never seem the same to me, now that I had seen what thunderbolts could strike us down. It is no wonder that we are taught the world and all its beauties are illusion.

After a while, the rain stopped and a wind rose in the pines. Little Yūshō became restless and he stamped around the room, stabbing at the dilapidated walls with his short sword. "Heh! Heh! I got you now! Hey, Yugiri, watch me fight."

Kiwako and Sōtōko began to cry again, softly. I looked at

Amaiko, but she showed no emotion at the mention of her husband's name.

"Mama, where is Yugiri? I want him to see how good I am. Heh! Heh!"

"Yugiri has . . . gone away, Yu-chan. Come sit down, please. You are making too much noise."

Yūshō plopped down beside Mama. "Where did he go?"

Mama put her arm around Yūshō. "He has gone to Mount Tai, where all the brave and the good go."

"Is it far?"

"Very far." I saw a tear fall on Mama's cheek.

"Will we go there, too?"

"Someday, Yu-chan."

There was silence again, except for Kiwako's and Sōtōko's weeping and the moaning of wind in the trees.

Amaiko sat bolt upright and stared at the outer wall. I jumped away from her, startled.

"Yugiri?" she said.

"Amaiko." I reached for her sleeve.

She leapt to her feet and ran to the shōji, shoving it aside. "Yugiri!"

I ran after her. She knocked aside two more doors and ran onto the veranda . . . where the boards were broken and rotting, and where the garden sloped sharply away down the mountainside.

"Yugiri!" she screamed.

I caught her kimono just before she reached the edge of the veranda. She still leaned forward, and I had to pull back on the cloth to keep us both from falling.

"Yugiri!" Amaiko's hands clawed the darkness as if to rend it, to reach something beyond it.

I looked but saw nothing except the dark shapes of the pines against the moonlit, clouded sky. "Amaiko, there is nobody here! Come back inside, please!"

In an instant she fell back against me, her face impassive as before. I carefully led her back to the central room; Amaiko walking as though in her sleep.

Mama looked up as we entered. "Is she all right?"

I did not know how to answer, so I said nothing. I helped Amaiko sit by the fire. She responded to my touch as though I were a puppeteer and she the puppet.

"Did she see his ghost?" asked Kiwako. She and Sōtōko stared at us as if Amaiko herself were a phantasm.

"I saw nothing," I said.

"But what did *she* see?" said Kiwako.

"That is enough talk of ghosts," said Mama. "We should all try to get some sleep."

"I won't sleep if she keeps jumping up like that," said Sōtōko.

Mama looked at me. "Stay by her, Mitsuko."

"Of course."

When we bedded down, Kiwako and Sōtōko slept far across the room from us. Little Yūshō curled up beside Mama. I slept beside Amaiko.

For a while, I doubted I could sleep at all. I kept remembering the attack—had it only been two days ago? It already seemed ages past. I wondered if things would have been different if Papa had been with us. Or would he now be dead, too? I wondered if Amaiko had truly seen Yugiri's ghost, and

if she would ever recover from her grief. Before long, however, I fell asleep.

I awoke with a start but saw nothing in the daylit room
that could have waked me. I ached all over. I knew my
dreams had been unquiet ones, though I did not remember
them. I remember hoping that all the horrible events of past
days had been a dream. My heart fell as I saw the stained
and warped shōji upon awakening.

I turned over to look at Amaiko. Her eyes stared, seeing
nothing. Fearing the worst, I shook her and called her name.
She breathed and allowed me to move her, but she still did
not respond to my words. And there was a smell.

I looked around, but no one else was nearby. I called in
the servants, and we cleaned Amaiko, and dressed Amaiko,
and fed Amaiko. When Kiwako and Sōtōko returned from
wherever they had been, they would not come near her. And
so it fell to me to be her nursemaid. I did not truly mind;
she had done so much for me in the past. I brushed her hair
and played the koto for her. I dressed her in the most fashionable style, as she had taught me. She allowed all of this,
but I could not tell if she knew I was there at all.

In the next days that passed, Mama sent the servants to
find whatever food they could from nearby farmers. What
they brought back were braces of rabbits and wild fowl, for
the soil in the mountains yielded little, but game was plen-
tiful. This made us all rather ill, as we are a Buddhist family
and were unused to eating meat.

Lord Tsubushima sent us a carpenter—a rough country fellow who mostly shook his head in dismay at the

impossibility of repairing the house. He turned out to be skilled in the making of soups, however, and he taught our servants how to make delicious broth with the meat, and the pine nuts we could find.

When the carpenter had to return to Lord Tsubushima, Mama sent a message to his Lord with him:

> *Our heads are now spared*
> *the rain from Heaven, though our*
> *sleeves still feel our tears.*
>
> *Please send a priest to ease our grief.*

In truth, though she would not tell us, Mama was becoming afraid. It had been nearly two weeks, and we had heard nothing from Papa. We could not send another servant to the capital—the road might still be dangerous and we had too few left to spare. Lord Tsubushima was not being very helpful. Now and then he would send messengers with invitations for us to move into his castle. Mama always sent them back with poems of polite refusal.

We were all afraid for Amaiko, and that was the true reason Mama had sent for a priest. "Grief is understandable," Mama said, "but this is beyond earthly sorrow."

Three days later, the priest finally arrived. He was old, and his eyes were rheumy, though he still had a vigorous stride. He wore the gray robes of a Buddhist monk, and so we were rather surprised when he took from a long box the branch of a sakaki tree and began to shake it around Amaiko.

"I am of a Shingon sect," he said in response to our wide stares. "What harm can there be in securing the goodwill of the kami, as well as the bodhisattvas? In these mountains, the people are closer to the spirits of the stones and trees than to the heavenly bringers of enlightenment. It does not shame me to say that I have offered sutras at many of the Shinto shrines in the forest, as well as set prayer wands at the foot of Kannon."

"Truly," said Mama, "we will be grateful for assistance, wherever it may come from."

"Take care what you say," the priest admonished her gently, "lest demons hear you. You do not want their help." He chanted a line from a sutra I did not recognize as he gazed at Amaiko's face. He lifted her hand, but when he let go, it dropped listlessly at her side.

"Is Amaiko possessed?" Kiwako whispered.

"Hush, do not bother him," said Mama.

"I am not bothered," said the priest. "Curiosity in the young is natural and good. No, my young Lady, I do not think your sister is possessed. Rather the opposite, in fact. She seems, instead . . . uninhabited. As if her soul has fled elsewhere."

"She has gone to join Yugiri," I said, though I hadn't meant to speak.

"Yugiri? Who is Yugiri?"

"Her husband," said Mama. "He was killed defending us from the wicked priests of Mount Hiei. I beg your pardon."

"I am not offended, Lady, save by those who do evil in holy robes. I am not of a warrior sect, and I myself wonder how such men can keep to a righteous path. I was told that much sorrow had visited this household, and now that I understand its source, perhaps I can, indeed, assist you."

I do not know exactly what the priest did then, for Mama

shooed us all from the room as he began his rituals. I only remember he was making a circle around Amaiko with crushed pine needles, while chanting the Sutra of Great Wisdom.

Feeling forlorn, I went out to the veranda, being careful not to sit on the broken wood. There I watched the clouded sky as it darkened toward nightfall, and wrote a poem.

> *Gray are the heavens,*
> *gray is the priest's robe,*
> *the color of ashes and death.*

And then a strange thing happened—it began to snow. A cold wind blew from the mountaintops, bringing white flakes dancing and swirling down the slopes. Before me, I saw moving forms among the whiteness, like invisible gosechi dancers. I pulled my kimonos tighter around me, torn between wonder and fear. The chanting of the priest within made the hair at my neck prickle.

He is summoning spirits, I thought, *hoping one of them will be Amaiko, returning to her body.* I shivered, wondering if I should have gotten a warding talisman from the priest to keep wandering spirits from possessing me.

I heard Mama calling.

A swirling column of snowflakes began to rise over the veranda. As it loomed over me, I thought I saw a face—I got up and ran inside.

"It's snowing!" I said as I joined the others at the hearth.

"Is it?" asked Mama.

"But it is only the Eighth Month!" exclaimed Kiwako.

"There must be storm demons in these mountains," said Sōtōko.

"I thought I saw a face among the snowflakes," I said softly to myself. No one appeared to hear me.

"Cold storms come early in this province," said the monk. "It is only somewhat earlier than usual." His name, we learned, was Dentō. He had joined us in the hearth room, but sat behind a screen for our modesty.

"How horrid," said Sōtōko.

"I want to go home," said Yūshō.

Mama sighed. "I hope we can soon."

I said to Dentō, "If I may ask, please, how is Amaiko?"

"I see no change in her," he replied. "Her spirit must be very far away. Perhaps she is, as you suggested, searching for her lost love."

"When will she come back?" asked Sōtōko.

"That is impossible to say."

"May I speak to Amaiko now?" I asked.

"As you wish. It will make no difference."

I did not again mention the shapes in the snow outside, for I did not want to seem foolish. Instead, I crept to the room where Amaiko sat.

She was a truly pitiable sight. Around her was a holy mandala painted in strange-smelling powders. Sakaki leaves stuck out from the folds of her kimonos and there was a smear of ashes on her forehead. As before, she stared at the floor and did not notice me. "Why won't you come back?" I said softly. "Can you not find him?"

A low moan arose from the wind in the pines outside.

"Why do you hurry toward death? Surely you and Yurigi were meant to be together and will meet again in your next lives?"

The wind rattled the doors and the roof tiles. My skin prickled and I covered my mouth. I knew I should not speak more of death, for it would attract unwholesome spirits. I felt many were about this night. I crawled into the mandala with Amaiko and held her hand. I laid my head upon her shoulder and I wept.

The monk Dentō stayed with us for several days. I think Mama was soothed by his presence and appreciated his chanting of the sutras for us. Before long, the air in the house was heavy with incense. I began to take Amaiko for walks around the veranda of the house so that we could breathe clear air.

The weather was still cold, and we saw neither sun nor moon. Patches of snow remained unmelted in the shadows of the trees. The leaves were beginning to turn on some of the trees and I was acutely aware of time passing. Were we missed back in the capital? Already the O-Bon Festival must have passed . . . Were our ancestors angry because we did not feast them this year? We would miss the moon-viewing parties and all the wonderful poetry written at them. I looked up at the sky, still veiled with a thin layer of clouds.

> *The moon has withdrawn*
> *behind a kichō of mist.*
> *Must she be so formal?*

> *Are others, elsewhere,*
> *welcomed in behind her screen*
> *as ardent lovers?*

> *I am jealous.*

It snowed lightly again three days later. On the day after that, a horseman arrived from Lord Tsubushima with a letter for Mama. We wondered what it could possibly contain, for Mama sat in long discussion with Dentō throughout the day. In the afternoon, when we gathered for the afternoon meal, we were amazed to see melon and strawberries on our plate.

"A gift from Lord Tsubushima," said Mama flatly.

We ate, very grateful. Little Yūshō, in particular, stuffed his mouth with abandon. I managed to feed a few bits to Amaiko.

When our plates were empty, Mama said, "Now that you are done, I will tell you the price of Lord Tsubushima's gift."

We looked at one another.

"In the letter I received today," she went on, "Lord Tsubushima says that his diviners tell him this will be a very cold autumn. He has heard that the monks of Mount Hiei are already scouring the land nearby, in search of whatever forage might help them through the winter. He says he has too few men to protect all of his province and it is all he can do to see that his own people will have enough this year. Lord Tsubushima urges us to move on to his castle, where he can provide adequate protection. After the grief we have suffered, he says it would wound him deeply if more disaster were to befall us."

"Can't we just go home?" said Kiwako.

Sōtoko nudged her with her elbow. "Didn't you hear her? She said the bad monks are still around."

"Does he say whether he has heard anything about what is going on in the capital?" I asked.

Mama said, "Only that he has heard very little, as the

passes are still dangerous. But he has heard there have been more fires, and there is still smoke over the city."

We all sighed in worry and sorrow.

"He also writes that he is eager to have women of good family and breeding in his castle—that there is much his people could learn from us as to the proper way of doing things. And that he has brave young sons who seek wives."

Sōtōko stared in horror at her. "Marry into a lower clan? Mama-chan, you could not ask us to!"

"The servants say these men are completely uncultured!" said Kiwako. "We could never return to the palace with such husbands!"

"Therefore," said Mama, drawing herself up, "it will be your task to teach them, so that we do not stain the reputation of the Fujiwara."

I could say nothing, I was so amazed at this turn of fate. I wondered what we had done in past lives that made us deserving of this ever increasing woe.

"It is truly not the future I had wished for you children," said Mama. "But we have been living on Lord Tsubushima's largesse for some time now, and without it we would perish. If fortune is with us, perhaps your father will be able to send word or come to us before anything irreversible occurs."

"Lord Tsubushima," said Dentō, from behind a screen, "is a man of great strength and ambition. He is very generous to his allies, but it is not wise to . . . disappoint him." He spoke sadly, as if from some personal experience.

Mama continued, "He has sent palanquins to us so that we may leave tomorrow. Let us pack what we have so we will be ready."

"What will happen to Amaiko?" I said.

Mama looked at her, then looked away. "I do not know."

But I did. As she was, Amaiko was completely unsuitable for marrying again. They would let her die.

It was then that I knew what I would do.

I could see the monk's shape faintly through the screen and I suddenly had the feeling he could see into my thoughts. I stared into the hearth coals, wondering what he would tell Mama. But she was busy consoling Kiwako and Sōtōko. As I rose to leave, I heard the monk softly summon me to his screen.

Uncomfortable, I crept over and said, "What do you wish?"

He reached under the screen and placed some sakaki leaves and a folded prayer-note into my hand. "I cannot offer you much protection, except to give you these. I will pray to Kannon to watch over and guide you, and to ask the kami of this land to keep you from harm."

Shaking, I placed the prayer and leaves into my right sleeve. "Thank you," I said. "You have been very kind to us."

"Kindness is not just for the sake of others," Dentō replied. "Enlightenment can come from humble service. Please be careful."

That afternoon, I obediently helped Mama pack. Then, in the evening, as twilight was falling, I took Amaiko out to the veranda. We walked slowly, as if taking a last look at this house that had lodged us in our sorrow. But from my many walks with her over the past days, I knew which part of the garden had the tallest weeds, and through which gate we could most quickly vanish from sight.

When I was certain no one was watching, I grabbed

Amaiko's hand and we descended into the weed-choked garden. I hurried as fast as I could to get us out of the compound and into the forest beyond.

It was madness, of course. I left with no plan, no direction, no preparations. I wanted only to get Amaiko away from there, so that she would not be taken by Lord Tsubushima's men.

As for myself, I did not care. I suppose I hoped that, after Mama and the others had left, we might return to the abandoned house and live there by ourselves. Are not the monotogari filled with stories of mysterious noblewomen living in decayed houses, waiting to be found by a wandering prince? I suppose I had imagined that we could live on air, as flowers do.

So, with no thoughts in my head, we plunged into the undergrowth of the forest. Again, a cold wind was blowing down from the mountaintops. Though I wore many layers of robes, they were summer garments, for we had thought our flight from the capital would be brief. My feet became wet from the frost on the ground, and the branches tore my fine sleeves, and I shivered in the chill. It was very dark, and I had no idea which way to go. I allowed Amaiko, who seemed to walk gracefully no matter where she was, to guide me by the way she leaned on my shoulders.

The tops of the trees above us roared in the wind. Suddenly Amaiko bumped against me and we stumbled onto a sort of path, much overgrown. We ran along it, as my shivering became greater and my teeth chattered like crickets. I began to realize how foolish I was, and I prayed that we might find some shelter soon.

After some time more of running, as I felt my breath was being drawn from my body by demons, I saw the path end at a low, dark building. We reached it much sooner than I expected; it turned out to be a miniature house. As we drew closer still, I saw it was a Shinto shrine. But, like the house we had just left, the shrine, too, was in terrible condition. Broken bits of pottery were the only offering on its steps and its walls leaned in at sad angles.

I scattered the pottery with a sweep of my hand, and pushing the tiny shōji aside, I crawled into the shrine, pulling Amaiko in with me. There was just enough room inside for the two of us to curl up tightly together, and with some effort I closed the shōji behind us.

It was much quieter inside, and my breathing and heartbeat seemed loud over the distant wind. The shrine smelled of stale incense and rotting wood. I held on to Amaiko for a long while and my shivering stopped, though I was still cold. I realized, when my mind calmed enough to think, that we were possibly committing a great sacrilege. This was meant to be a kami's house, after all. I wondered if the kami had abandoned it, or if the place had been forgotten by its worshipers. I pulled the sakaki leaves and the prayer from my sleeve and pushed them edgewise in between the tiny roof beams.

"Please forgive us," I said, in case the kami might be watching. "In the name of Kageru, who watches over the Fujiwara clan, I humbly request shelter and sanctuary for this night. We are lost and in need of aid. If you help us, I swear I shall see this shrine is repaired and not forgotten. If you choose not to help us, I ask only that you not harm us, for we mean no sacrilege. May the Amida bless you and guide you to the Path." I nestled back against Amaiko and rested my head on her shoulder.

As the night deepened, I wondered if we might die here. *Well,* I thought, *better here than shamefully in Lord Tsubu-shima's castle.* Amaiko would be free to join Yugiri in some future life, and the turn of the Wheel might offer me a life in which I could be more than the "little puddle" I was.

After some time, I slept. In my dreams, I felt we were floating, two lotus blossoms adrift on a river.

I do not know how much later I awoke. Something was wrong. The shōji was open, revealing a dark shape. Someone was staring in at us.

Little Sister of Water

A leaf adrift on
Lake Biwa: "How wide this stream
is! Where is the shore?"

*M*Y HEART POUNDED like a drum. "Are you the kami of this shrine?" was all I could think to say.

"I was going to ask you the same question," said whatever-it-was, "so clearly we are both mistaken." Its voice was like that of an old man, or a raven trained to speak.

I struggled to sit up and I bumped my head on the rafters of the little shrine. Sakaki leaves and the prayer Dentō had written for me rained down into my lap.

The thing at the door gasped and stepped back into a shaft of moonlight. I nearly gasped myself, for I saw it was the face of a huge black bird with human eyes.

A *tengu!* I thought, wondering if I should be more afraid.
I had heard that these shape-shifters of the mountain forests
were sometimes friendly to man, but sometimes cruel. Some
say the tengu drink blood through their long beaks. Some say
they bring gifts on happy occasions. I did not know what to
expect.

"What is it?" I heard another voice outside the shrine.

"I have found human children," said the tengu.

"Oh, excellent!" said the other. "Shall we eat them? Shall
we play with them?"

I became angry then. "Who are you to peep in on us?"

"Who are *you* to usurp a kami's house?" said the tengu.

"It looked abandoned and we needed shelter."

"Have you no home of your own?"

I paused. "No. Not anymore." Sadness swept over me like
a cold wind and I curled up against Amaiko's shoulder.

"Well, then, who are you? What are your names?"

The tengu's impertinence cut through my sorrow. "This
is Fujiwara no Amaiko, and I am her little sister." Surely
everyone had heard of Amaiko.

"What did she say?" croaked one of the other tengu.

"Oh, ho!" said the first. "We have found nobility! Are the
Good People of the capital no longer content to live Above
the Clouds, that they desire the houses of gods?"

Harsh laughter rattled among the trees outside.

"Stop that!" I said. "You have no right to be so unkind."

"No right?" said the tengu. "You are bold, Little Sister of
Amaiko, to make such a claim. Do you have a name of your
own?"

"Though I cannot possibly see how it matters, I am
Mitsuko."

" 'Fourth Daughter'? How poetic. Wait . . . aren't you the one they call Little Puddle at the Palace?"

I buried my face in my sleeves out of shame. What karma in my past lives had earned me such humiliation?

"I am honored to meet you," the tengu went on.

"There is no need to mock me so."

"No, truly. You are known to be kind and clever. Whatever has brought you and your sister to this forest?"

Words tumbled out of me, unwise though it seemed. "We had to flee the capital because monks from Mount Hiei were going to burn our house down. But on the road, the monks attacked us—" At this, I heard the tengu draw in his breath. I did not know what this meant, so I went on. "Amaiko's husband was killed. And the monks stole our goods. When we reached our refuge, it was in ruins. And now Lord Tsubushima won't help us unless we marry his sons. And I don't know if my father is alive. And Amaiko has lost her soul. So I ran away and brought her with me. We found this shrine and took shelter here. I have asked the kami of this shrine to aid us."

It was silent outside. And then the tengu said, "You are very brave, Little Puddle. Monks from Mount Hiei, you say? And Lord Tsubushima? Well, well. It would seem the kami has answered both our prayers."

"What do you mean?"

"You have prayed to the kami for assistance. Just this evening, I prayed to my clan kami for diversion. It seems we will both get what we asked for."

My stomach tightened. "Diversion?"

"Surely you know we tengu are no friends to monks. It is our greatest pleasure to torment them, in fact. Monks have done you ill; therefore we are duty bound to assist and avenge you. Come out and let us meet you properly."

"How—how do we know that we can trust you?"

"A good question, Little Puddle. How do we know that we may trust *you*?"

This confused me. I could not see what possible harm I could do them, and I told him so.

"Often those weapons that are most easily hidden can cause the worst pain. Come out so that we may see you are hiding no weapons in there."

This utter nonsense irritated me. "Very well. We'll come out and you can see how ridiculous you are being." Gently, I helped Amaiko out of the shrine. Her skin was cold, and she could hardly stand.

I looked up and saw before me four or five ravenlike tengu as tall as I was, wearing bright-colored sleeveless jackets over their wings.

The one who had been speaking to us bowed to me. "I am Goranu," he said.

I bowed as much as I could while holding on to Amaiko.

"What is wrong with the big one?" said one of the other tengu. His voice was like the splitting of wood when a branch is broken.

"I told you," I said. "Her soul is wandering, searching for the spirit of her husband."

Goranu tilted his head and regarded her. "Ai, she does not look well at all. If we do not hurry, she may have no body to return to. Come, we will take you both to our village, where you will be warm and your sister cared for."

I realized that my legs hurt and I felt weak from cold. "Is your village near? I don't think we can walk far."

All of the tengu laughed again, making sounds like the clattering of bamboo slats. "Ho, Little Puddle, it is not near, yet you need not walk at all!"

"Forgive me, but I am not in the mood for riddles," I grumbled as I shivered.

"Then I will not keep you waiting for the answer." Goranu rattled at his fellow tengu and they came forward, bearing something long and pale between their beaks. They jerked their heads in unison and flung out a large rope net before us.

Goranu nodded at the net. "It is not so fancy as a carriage, my Ladies, but your journey will be swifter than on horse-back, and smoother than on a boat at sea. Step in, if you please."

I guided Amaiko onto the net and we sat. I had many misgivings.

> A net appears to
> pull me to another world.
> Is this how fish feel
> as they become guests of the fishermen?

The tengu cawed and clattered again at one another, and each stepped onto the edge of the net. Goranu said, "Ready, up!" and every tengu began furiously flapping his wings. The wind this created whipped Amaiko's hair into my face and I couldn't see anything.

The net stretched up around us and suddenly we were pulled into the air. I cried out, I think, and grabbed on to the net tightly with one hand. With the other I held Amaiko. Her face showed no change of expression.

When I gathered the courage to look around, I was

amazed to see how high we were. The forested slopes below us were like heaped cushions of the blackest silk, darker than Amaiko's hair. The sky was enormous and ablaze with stars . . . I had never seen so many . . . as if the greatest festival of all, with candles and lanterns and torches, were going on there. I could dimly see the jagged peaks of the highest mountains in the distance, wearing patches of snow that glimmered in the starlight. *Is this how the gods see the world?* I wondered. *How fortunate they are!*

The tengu turned and our net swung around to face a different direction. Ahead of us I could see a mountain on which many torches flickered. There were large buildings, and I could not tell if they were temples or palaces.

"Goranu," I yelled up to the tengu, "what is that place?"

"Ah," he called back, "that is Mount Hiei, Little Puddle. Home of your enemies."

I clutched the net tightly. For a moment I wished I truly were a god, and did not just have the vantage point of one. I wished I could reach out my fist and pound the buildings below me into shards, sending the tiny priests scattering like ants. Amida forgive me for such a hateful thought, but it was so.

As we flew closer, the buildings loomed larger, and I became afraid. "Goranu, aren't we getting too close?"

"Fear not, Little Puddle."

And at that, the tengu turned again. Our net swung beneath them, and now we faced a huge cliff in the side of the mountain. We drew closer and closer and I feared we were going to be smashed against the rock face. Then I saw one of the shadows in the cliff was an opening just large enough for us to fly through.

In a moment we were on the other side. Below us was a valley in which a tiny village lay. We circled lower and lower. I did not see how they could alight on the ground without hurting us. I held tightly on to Amaiko and moaned into her shoulder. I prayed to Amida, Kannon, Kageru, or whoever might listen, to come to our aid.

I heard above me the heavy flapping of the tengu's wings and felt their wind in my hair. To my amazement, the net gently brushed the ground, and then we were lying safely still, with solid earth beneath us.

I looked up. We were in the middle of a commoners' village of thatched wooden huts such as one sees on the way to the Inari shrine. I heard a rumbling noise and saw women running out of the huts toward us. What strange creatures they were! They had long noses like beaks, and hunched backs. Their fingers were like talons and their feet were flat and hideous. They came running up to us and stared.

"What have you brought us?" they cawed. "Are they food? Are they playthings? What pretty clothes they have!"

"Peace!" said Goranu. "These are Fujiwara noblewomen from the capital. They have been wronged by the priests of Mount Hiei and therefore are our guests. Treat them with kindness and respect, if you please."

The tengu women made disappointed noises but bowed to us in a curious bobbing fashion. I sat up and helped Amaiko to sit up also. I tried to stand, but my legs shook beneath me and I could not.

Immediately, many hands took my arms and shoulders. I was lifted and carried to one of the huts, as was Amaiko, beside me. I was too tired and cold to resist, though I was afraid. Inside the hut, a fire was crackling in the central hearth. An iron pot hung over the fire. Amaiko and I were put on straw mats beside the hearth, where it was deliciously warm. We were each given bowls of bean soup. I helped Amaiko eat a little, which surprised the tengu women.

"What is wrong with her?" they asked.

"Her soul is away, searching for her husband," Goranu said.

They cawed and clucked sympathetically, patting Amaiko's arm. I wanted to brush them all away, but I dared not give offense.

After we ate, I could hardly stay awake. I lay down beside Amaiko and drifted off into a warm, dreamless slumber.

When I awoke, I scarcely knew where I was. At first, I imagined I was home in Heian Kyō — but the smells were all wrong. I opened my eyes and saw the rough earthen wall of a hut instead of the fine, stained walls of the ruined mountain lodge. Then I realized the tengu had not been a dream and I sat up.

Amaiko was gone.

I was alone. Coals still glowed in the hearth, and dim sunlight shone beyond the doorway, but there was no one in sight. I listened and heard only the songs of distant birds and my own breathing.

"Good morning!" I called out, my voice uncertain. "Please show yourselves! I would like some breakfast, please." I thought I heard movement somewhere nearby, but no one replied. I crawled to the doorway and looked outside. The entire village seemed deserted. "Hello! Good morning! Where is everybody?"

"Shhh! Stop yelling, Little Puddle!" I heard behind me. A large black bird was entering through a cloth-covered doorway at the back of the hut.

"Goranu? Where is everyone? Where is Amaiko?"

"We tengu often sleep during the day. So, if you please, don't make so much noise."

"But where is Amaiko?"

"Hush. Do not worry. She is safe."

"Let me see her then."

"Not right now."

"Yes, now!" I flung myself at him and beat against his upraised wings with my fists. "Where is Amaiko? Take me to her!"

"Ow! Ow! Stop it! Don't you want to help her?"

I stopped and sat in frustration. "Of course I do."

"Then listen. I have been thinking about this. If your sister has gone seeking her husband's soul, then we must search for him in order to find her."

"How can we possibly do that?" I said. "The monk Dentō has tried the Rite of Souls' Return and it failed."

"Monk? Pah!" Goranu ruffled his feathers. "I am a *tengu!* We can do better than monk's magic. As the saying goes, the Mountain of Death is no barrier to the cuckoo—and I am no mere bird, either."

"Well, what are we going to do then?"

"We are going to ask the advice of my friend the Dragon King."

"Dragon King?" I had heard tales about dragons, and I knew they were powerful and wise, but also dangerous. "On what mountain is this dragon?"

"Oh, no. Dragons live in water, not on mountaintops. Every body of water has its dragon, from Lake Biwa, to the Kamo River, to the smallest puddle." Goranu gave me a knowing look. "But my friend is the greatest of them all, the Dragon King of the Sea. Often he receives souls of the dead in his palace, and perhaps he has seen this what's-his-name of your sister's."

"Koga no Yugiri."

"Yes, him. Or some soul who knows his fate."

"Are you sure a great king will help us?"

"Of course he will! Did I not say I am an old friend of his? And he owes me a favor. I rescued a cousin or niece of his some time ago. But then his relatives are always in need of rescue. They keep crawling out of their safe waters in the form of worms or snakes. I think that's the only way His Majesty meets people. So, are you willing to make the journey?"

"I want to see Amaiko first."

Goranu sighed. "You are a stubborn one. Very well. Come with me."

I followed him out of the hut and into the cottage next door. There Amaiko sat, her face still expressionless as a doll's. Tengu women were brushing her hair and arranging her clothing.

"So. You see? She is being cared for."

I sat on a straw mat near her. I did not like the way one tengu woman stroked Amaiko's silken sleeve, as if desiring such finery herself. But, again, I dared not give offense. "Anything that will help Amaiko," I said softly, "I will do."

"Good. Now eat your breakfast and we will be off."

Goranu picked up a wooden bell in his beak and rattled it. Another tengu woman shuffled in, rubbing her eyes with one hand. In the other, she carried a tray with a bowl of rice and some pickled vegetables. As I picked at the rice, she brushed my hair and tugged my kimonos into place. I wished I could shoo her away.

"Hurry, hurry!" said Goranu.

"Why must we rush so?"

"To catch the winds! The lifting sea breeze begins an hour after dawn, and we must be away by then. A very long journey lies ahead of us."

I was brought a long-handled basket filled with rice balls, dried meat, and vegetables. The handle was draped over my shoulder. I went to Amaiko and held her hand. "Good-bye, Sister. When we meet again, I hope to see you smile."

Nothing in her face changed to show she had heard me. Disappointed, I let go of her hand and I followed Goranu outside. At first I hid my face behind my sleeves, but then I felt foolish. There was no one but Goranu to look at me.

"Where will we find this Dragon King of the Sea?" I said.

"Far away, Little Puddle, on the island of Enoshima, in Sagami Bay. That is where the Dragon King lives." Stretching out his wings, Goranu lowered himself to the ground. "Now get on my back."

"Oh, no! I could not—however would I stay on?"

"Grab hold of my feathers, foolish one. Hurry!"

I tried to swallow my fear. The many layers of kimonos I wore, and the basket I carried, made the climb difficult, but at last I was able to pull myself onto his back between his wings.

"Very good. Now hold on!" He began to run to the other

end of the village, flapping his wings furiously. I had to bury my face in his neck feathers so as not to get beaten about the head. I felt him jump into the air and I clenched my hands in his feathers.

After a while, he was not flapping so hard and I dared to look around. I gasped in amazement at what I saw. It was as though we had fallen into the most beautiful screen painting. The sun had risen, illuminating the western mountains. The slopes seemed afire with the reds and golds of autumn leaves. Goranu spiraled up and up, until the hillsides below seemed like the carelessly discarded brocade robe of some mighty emperor. I almost forgot to be afraid. Then the wind caught Goranu's wing, tilting him, and I nearly fell off.

I clutched his feathers and the skin beneath them very hard after that. "Why are we flying so high?" I asked when I could again speak.

"To fly over the mountains, Little Puddle. You will see."

I looked around and saw behind and to our right the glittering of many tile roofs. "Goranu, is that the capital?"

"You are very perceptive. Yes, that is Heian Kyō."

How my heart leaped toward those tiled roofs. Papa was there. Home was there. "Turn around, Goranu! You must take me to Heian Kyō! I must see my father!"

"No, no, I cannot! If I turn west, we will be fighting the winds and we will get nowhere. Besides, if we delay, Amaiko will die, no matter what your father does. We must continue."

Tears blurred my vision of the shining rooftops and I felt as if part of me was being torn away. I buried my face in Goranu's black feathers and wept. He flew onward, uncaring.

But I could not cry forever, and presently curiosity forced

me to raise my head. A mountain crest dusted with snow was passing just beneath us. Goranu used no effort at all now, just holding his wings out to catch the wind. We glided back and forth above the mountain slopes. Then I saw ahead of us a vast expanse of water, like a cloak of gray-green silk, shimmering in the morning sun.

"Goranu, is that the sea?"

"Taking an interest in our surroundings once more, are you? No, Little Puddle, that is Lake Biwa, famous in song and legend."

"But it is so . . . big!"

"So it is. But not nearly as big as the sea."

I had thought Lake Biwa might only be as wide as the lake on the Palace grounds, where the Emperor at times would have his dragon boats rowed out to view the moon. "The world is much wider than I thought," I said softly.

"A valuable lesson to learn," said Goranu. "You know, a fellow tengu told me that there is a brook that empties into Lake Biwa, whose burbling is the chanting of the Buddha's teaching."

"Truly?"

"He says the waters are so holy because they flow from the privies of the temples on Mount Hiei."

I pulled one of his feathers.

"Ow!"

"That is for teasing me. And I don't think you should say such impious things."

"I'm a tengu! Impiety is my nature. But I will be more careful in what I say to you. I need all the feathers I have."

Despite myself, I laughed.

I am sure even pilgrims do not travel as far as we did that day. We skimmed low over rivers, startling the fishermen as they placed their screenlike nets in the water. We flew high up the mountainsides, letting the warm breath of the mountain kami lift us high, high into the air. Then we would dive again into the next mountain valley. At times, we would stop at waterfalls to refresh ourselves.

Goranu would talk to the fish in the streams. He would say, "Hello, Brother Carp! Seen any fat monks lately? Say, you look just like the Abbot of Tenryukuji! Did some angry kami transform you, Your Holiness?" I thought it quite comical.

I had nearly forgotten our purpose, so overwhelmed was I by all I had seen on our journey. But I began to weary in the afternoon. If the world was so wide, how could we possibly find one soul in it, or in the worlds beyond?

At one of our stops to rest, I said, "We have gone so far, Goranu. When do we get to the sea?"

"It is yet a way, Little Puddle," said Goranu. "Look in the basket you were given — there should be food there for you."

"Ah, yes, I remember." I took out a rice cake and nibbled on it. As soon as I finished it, I no longer felt so weary, and I said so.

"That is tengu magic," said Goranu, proudly puffing out the feathers on his chest. "Now climb once more on my back, for there are wonders yet to see."

I did not think anything could be more wondrous than all we had already seen, but I was wrong. How little I knew of the world! I climbed again onto Goranu's back and we again leaped into the air. We skimmed through a high mountain pass and suddenly I understood. Before us, in the distance, was the most perfect mountain I had ever seen, a plume of smoke drifting up from its summit.

"Goranu," I whispered, "is that Fuji-sama?"

"It is indeed the Sacred Mountain, Little Puddle. Keep your eye upon her, for she marks our way."

I recognized it from paintings I had seen, yet no painting could capture its true beauty. *Surely birds are the most fortunate of animals*, I thought, *to be blessed with such visions.*

"It is said," Goranu went on, "that Fuji-sama rose during an earthquake, and that once there was a mountain higher than she, but she jealously pounded it to bits."

"Truly?"

"And that plume of smoke? That is a box of burning incense. The name of the incense is Recall of the Soul — we could use some of that, neh? Anyway, the box was set afire by the love of a provincial governor who married the spirit of the mountain when she took human form."

"You are teasing me again. But I can see why pilgrims endure so much to visit her."

"Would you like me to set you down on her flanks? We'll be passing quite near her."

"Oh, no! I couldn't! I haven't been through the hundred-day purification! Besides, I'm a girl. Women are not permitted to set foot on the Sacred Mountain."

"Who says so?"

"All the holy ones do."

"Monks. Pah! What do they know? All the more reason I should set you there."

"Please don't. I fear I have already lost my chance at a

better rebirth by being in your company. I should not make matters worse."

"Well! Thank you so very much, Madame Wisteria-Choked Puddle! Perhaps I should just drop you here and let you fly yourself home."

"No, no—please forgive me! I meant no offense!"

"Heh. Just watch your manners when we meet the Dragon King. He's very fussy that way."

"I will remember." I buried my face in my sleeves and said nothing more. After a while, I peered out again. The sun was setting, and Fuji-sama glowed crimson-gold.

The mountain's shape made me think of my mother kneeling, weeping. I wondered if Mama missed me. Were she and my sisters searching for Amaiko and me? I even wished I could hear Kiwako and Sōtōko's stupid laughter again. My running away now seemed very foolish.

> So far from the Path
> I should be on, I stray
> into unknown lands.
>
> O sacred Fuji,
> may your holy fires and smoke
> safely guide me home.

We flew low beside a wide river until a warm wind lifted us. "Feel that?" said Goranu. "That is the seaward breeze— the last wind we must catch before our destination. But we must be careful, and beware of the winds from Fuji's slopes, or she will catch us and sweep us far out of our way."

I did not know what to make of Goranu's words, so I said

nothing. Ahead of us was a great blue-gray darkness stretching away to the end of the world. *That*, I thought, *must be the sea.* It was, indeed, much greater than Lake Biwa. I felt very small and insignificant, and suddenly feared meeting the monarch of All That.

"Hold on!" said Goranu, and he tilted sideways as we turned, following the shore of Sagami Bay. I grabbed on to the feathers just below his neck. I am sure my pinching must have hurt him, but he showed no sign of it as we flew very, very fast. Lower and lower we dropped, toward the beach, and I feared we would dash ourselves against the sand. We skimmed over the water, just behind the waves, so low that a fish could have jumped up and joined me on Goranu's back.

He tilted up and began to beat his wings hard. I had to fling my arms around his neck to keep from falling off. Then he bounced and I saw he was running along a narrow strand. At last he stopped.

He took a deep breath and said, "Welcome to Enoshima, Little Puddle. You may get off now."

I slid down his outstretched wing to the sand. The sun had set, and stars already were appearing in the purple sky. The waves gently lapped against the island's shore, their foam glowing a faint green. I asked Goranu about the strange froth.

"That is the Dragon King's magic."

I turned. Up on a hill was a shrine. "Is that to the kami of the island or to the sea?"

"I would not know. Oh, look! A giant sea turtle!"

"Where?" I peered hard at the waves curling onto the shore, but because of the darkness, I could see nothing. I turned to Goranu to ask again where the turtle was — and saw an old man in a black robe standing there.

I immediately held my sleeves up to my face. "Please pardon me, Venerable Sir. Have you seen — ?" I paused, wondering if he would think me mad for asking after a huge black bird.

The old man laughed. "I am Goranu, you silly girl." His voice was the same. "We tengu change shape, remember? But we are also modest and do not like being watched, and that is why I distracted you."

"Oh. Is that your real shape?"

The old man Goranu scowled at me. "Now you are being insulting again."

"Forgive me. It seems I do not know what may give insult to a tengu."

"So. You are learning, neh? Come, we must go this way."

I followed him to the end of the island that pointed out into the bay. Behind us, up on the hillside, was a shallow cave. Goranu guided me to it and said, "You may rest here until the Dragon King comes."

I knelt in the cave and found the floor to be a bed of soft sand. I considered a moment and turned to Goranu. "You must not think, though I am far from home and at your mercy, that you can take advantage of me here."

In the dim twilight I saw Goranu stare, aghast. "What sort of creature do you take me for? We tengu are not like the badger or the fox, who change shape to lure humans into marriage. For that matter, we are not like rapacious men, either. In that regard, Little Puddle, you are safe with me, never fear."

I nodded and curled up on the sand. Yet I wondered if we mortals had as bad a reputation among demons as they had among us.

Goranu pulled from somewhere a flute and began to play a haunting melody. I was so tired, and the music made me feel so curiously at peace, that I fell asleep almost at once.

In the middle of the night, I awoke—at least, I believe I did. The sea was much higher, the waves coming almost up to the cave mouth. The waves themselves were larger, the foam spraying high. In their green glow, I perceived the manes and whiskers and snouts of great dragons splashing in the surf.

"Get up, Little Puddle," said Goranu. "The Dragon King is coming!"

I slowly rose to my knees and crept to the mouth of the cave. Presently, out of the waves strode a bearded old man in glowing robes. He scowled beneath his heavy brows, as if that were his usual expression. He wore a crown with a golden serpent on it, and in one hand he held an enormous pearl or moonstone. I bowed, placing my forehead against the cool, wet sand.

"Greetings, mighty Ryujin!" Goranu said.

"Goranu. You have returned so soon." The Dragon King's voice was like the thunder of the waves and the hissing of the sea foam. I trembled to hear it.

"Ah, it has actually been two years, Majesty. But I know time is not the same in your kingdom."

"That is, indeed, so," said the Dragon King. "Well, then. Why have you summoned me?"

"You said, at our parting, that should I ever need a favor from you, I need only blow on this flute and ask."

"I did, good Goranu. What favor would you ask?"

"Actually, I ask on behalf of another."

The Dragon King boomed out a laugh. "How un-tengu-like of you, Goranu. For what worthy soul do you make your petition?"

"Permit me to introduce Fujiwara no Mitsuko. Also known as Little Puddle. It is she who requires your help." I felt Goranu tug on my sleeve. "Say something!" he whispered.

"Honored Majesty . . ." I began, but I found myself unable to speak further. I looked helplessly at Goranu.

"I know your kinsmen well, Lady of the Fujiwara," said King Ryujin to me. "They have been helpful to my family several times. And your name speaks well of you. Many of my relatives find their homes in ponds and puddles. I will be pleased to aid you, if I can. Come with me and we may discuss the matter in my palace."

"No!" said Goranu. "Er, that is, with no offense to Your Majesty, our task has some urgency to it. Were we to visit your kingdom, though it might seem we were gone but an hour, centuries might pass here in the mortal lands."

"I think you exaggerate," said the Dragon King. "Besides, if you pass the time away in my kingdom, the problem will likely have solved itself."

"While the passage of decades may mean nothing to a demon such as I am, I believe this unfortunate mortal is still sentimental about this world of illusion and hopes to see her family once again. Therefore we must decline your hospitable offer, most Generous Majesty."

"Very well," grumbled King Ryujin. "For what urgent matter do you seek my counsel?"

"We are looking for someone."

"Someone you expect me to have seen?"

"Precisely."

"And who is this urgently sought person?"

Goranu tugged my sleeve again.

"We seek my sister's husband," I blurted out. "Koga no Yugiri."

"Hmmm . . ." The Dragon King put a long-nailed hand to his chin. "The name is not familiar. Did he rescue one of my children?"

"No, Majesty," said Goranu. "He is dead."

"Ah. Did he die at sea?"

"No, Majesty, he was killed near Mount Hiei, by monks of Enriyaku-ji Temple."

"Well, I confess I do not see why you are asking me about him."

"He is a cousin of the Emperor, as I understand it. You sometimes receive the souls of nobility, don't you?"

"Well, that depends upon circumstances. I would remember a cousin of the Emperor, but I have seen no such personage recently."

"Ah, a pity," said Goranu. "I should have known it would not be so simple."

"But you have whetted my curiosity," said the Dragon King. "Why do you pursue this dead nobleman? Why not let him seek his new life in peace?"

Goranu looked at me.

"Because, O mighty King," I said, "my sister . . . his wife . . . her soul has gone in search of him, though her body yet lives. If I can find him, I might find her as well. Or somehow learn a way to bring her back to herself."

"This is curious, indeed," said King Ryujin. "You must love your sister very much to undertake such a search for her."

"Yes, Majesty," I whispered, near tears again. "That is so."

"Hmmm. I know of an island named Miiraku where you can view the dead from a distance. However, if you approach, the vision will vanish."

"That would not be of use to us, Majesty," said Goranu.

"Mmmm, I suppose not. Well, then, as I see it, you have no other choice but to speak with Lord Emma-o himself."

"I was hoping we could avoid that," said Goranu.

"Ho, ho! Is a tengu showing trepidation?" said the King. "Why, *she*"—he pointed at me—"has much more to fear than you."

"It is for her that I fear."

"Naturally." King Ryujin smiled. "I suppose you will want me to open the way for you?"

"If Your Majesty would be so kind."

"At least I shall not have come all this way for nothing." The Dragon King bent down to me. His breath smelled strongly of fish. "It was pleasant to meet you, Child of the Fujiwara. Please accept this gift from me. Use it when you find an opportunity." He pulled from a fold within his robes a black pearl as large as my thumb, and placed it in my hand.

I could scarcely speak to express my gratitude. I bowed very low once more.

"Goranu," the Dragon King said, "I cannot discern why you have chosen to display such kindness and generosity to a mortal—"

"Perhaps I do not wish to be a tengu in all my future lives, Majesty."

"A noble goal. I wish you well. Good night to you both then."

The Dragon King of the Sea waved the hand that had held the pearl in a circle toward the cave. He turned and walked back into the surf. The dragons sporting in the waves turned as he entered the water, and they sank out of sight behind him. The waves thundered as he disappeared into their midst. Then the sea became calm. All was as it had been when we arrived.

"So" — Goranu sighed — "we had best be going. The way will not stay open long."

"What way? Where are we going?"

"Haven't you been paying attention? *That* way." He pointed back toward the cave.

I turned. It was no longer a shallow grotto. The back of the cave was now a great gaping hole, filled with darkness.

Little Sister of Fire

*The incense burns with
unseen fire; what hidden flames
smolder in my soul?*

$\mathcal{G}$ORANU GRABBED my sleeve and pulled me into the dark cavern. As we entered, there was a thunderous boom and the rock wall closed behind us, cutting off even the dim moonlight. Only blackness surrounded us.

"What shall we do?" I asked. I confess I was very afraid.

Goranu caused a pale blue flame to appear in the palm of his hand. It illuminated very little of the cave around us. "For now," he said, yawning, "I am going to get some sleep."

"Sleep? Here? Now?"

He frowned at me. "I have just flown over two hundred ri, played the flute for hours to summon King Ryujin, and

73

argued with him on your behalf. I think I am entitled to some rest. *You* may do whatever you wish." He dropped to the sandy cave floor and pulled his jacket over his head. He looked very much like a bird covering itself with its wing. The little blue flame in his hand went out.

"Goranu?"

He answered with a snore.

What could I do? I could see nothing. So I sat where I stood. *What creatures might lurk in this cave?* I wondered. I felt no wind, heard no sound other than Goranu's noisy breathing. *Well,* I thought at last, *he would not be sleeping so if there were any danger.* I curled up beside him and tried to rest as well.

I had no way of knowing how much later I woke up. I had dreamed of waterfalls and awoke needing to do a necessary thing. I blinked to be sure I was not still dreaming, but the cave now was lit with a dim red glow. I carefully got up, so as not to wake Goranu. I walked toward the light. I saw a semicircle of large rocks and went among them.

Just as I finished and rearranged my robes, I heard a man's deep voice humming. It seemed to be coming from farther down the cave. I peered out from behind a rock and was amazed. There stood a man much taller than anyone I had ever seen. He had a mane of bright orange hair and a thick orange beard. He wore only a loincloth, and a band around his forehead. He carried a large drum under each arm. He set the drums on a bamboo rack that already held other drums of different sizes. Beside the rack was a post with two clamshells atop it. When the man pushed a lever at the bottom of the post with his foot, the clamshells clacked together. He laughed when he did this, clearly thinking himself very clever.

Then he took from beside the wall a cloth-headed mallet, which he tapped against the smallest drum. It made a sound like the soft booming of the sea waves. He chuckled. He tapped a larger drum. Its voice was like nearby thunder, and a bit of dirt trickled down from the ceiling. He tapped an even larger drum, and the earth shook around me with a rumble I felt in my bones. Rocks rained down from above me. He laughed and pulled back the mallet, aiming for the largest drum—

"Ai, no!" I cried out.

He stopped and sniffed the air. "Who is there?" His voice was like stones grinding together.

I ducked behind the rock, wishing I could speak to Goranu. Surely the noise must have woken him.

"I smell a mortal," the creature continued. "You'd best come out, little human. You have no way to escape."

There was nothing else to do. I covered my face with my sleeves and crept out from behind the rock.

"Oh, ho! A girl child, and wealthy, from the look of her! What are you doing here?"

"Please do not hurt me," I said.

"Well, now, that depends," he said, coming closer. "You had better have a good reason to be here. Be quick to tell me."

"The Dragon King, Ryujin, let us in."

"Us? There are more of you? Why would Ryujin-sama want to put pretty girls into the Cave of Fuji?"

I did not answer. I looked around. *Where is Goranu?* I wondered.

The fellow came up and sat cross-legged before me. "Come, now. You have made me put off my practice. You must make it up to me with your story. It had better be interesting."

"We are searching for my sister's husband's soul."

"In here? And where is your pretty companion?"

"My companion is a tengu, and he is back that way."

"A tengu? This *is* becoming interesting. But it had better be the truth."

"I assure you, it is."

"Then tell me more."

Not knowing what else to do, I quickly blurted my whole tale to him. He listened with his chin in his hand.

"You are lucky," he said when I had finished. "You must love your sister very much. My sister and I do not get along so well." He winked at me. "But why have you come searching in here?"

"I do not know. The Dragon King said we must speak to Lord Emma-o."

The creature rocked back and laughed so loud the cave walls shook.

"Please stop that," I said, covering my head.

He grinned and sat still. "Forgive me. I sometimes forget how fragile mortals are. Tell me, did King Ryujin give you anything?"

I wondered if he knew of the black pearl I had been given. The Dragon King had told me I should use it when an opportunity arose. But I did not know if this was the time.

"Come, now," said the fellow. "Try to remember. Did he?"

It was clear that my interrogator was some sort of god or demon. I knew I was not clever enough to outwit him. Certainly it would have been unwise to try. I reached into my sleeve and pulled out the black pearl.

He snatched it from my hand and held it up before his eyes. "Ahhh! Such a beauty! King Ryujin knows my tastes well. I must add it to my collection." He dropped the pearl into a fold in his loincloth.

"May it give you pleasure," I said softly. Had I just been unfairly robbed? I dared not insult such a powerful personage.

I heard a strange whimper behind me and I turned. Goranu was crawling toward us, moaning.

"Goranu, what is wrong?" I said to him.

He did not look at me. He kept his eye fixed firmly on the ground as he said, "O Impetuous One, O Ancestor of My Ancestors, forgive us for not recognizing you and doing you proper obeisance!"

Suddenly understanding, I flung myself down and pressed my forehead to the ground. "What god or lord is he?" I whispered to the tengu.

Goranu did not answer me directly. "O Master of the Storm and Earthquake, Brother to She Who Is the Sun, have patience with us!"

The name came to me then. *Susano-wo. Brother to Amataseru.* I trembled inside. I had never thought I would meet such a powerful and ancient kami. I prayed to Kannon for protection—but I wondered if a bodhisattva had any power over one of the elder kami. It was not a matter mentioned in the sutras or at temple festivals.

Susano-wo was chewing a fingernail. "You are becoming tiresome, O Descendant of One of My More Ill-Considered Acts. Fortunately, your charming companion has paid for your passage. She was just telling me a story."

Goranu sat upright. There was something wrong with his face, and his black robe seemed to be sprouting feathers. "A skilled tale teller, is she not, O Grandfather of My Grandfathers?" To me he whispered, "What have you told him?"

I slowly sat up also. "Only the truth. I have told him that we search for Yugiri's soul."

"An interesting tale, is it not, O Rescuer of Mortal Maidens?"

"So far," said Susano-wo.

"And he has taken — that is, I have given him the Dragon King's pearl."

"A beautiful gem, is it not, O Provider of the Sacred Jewel?"

"Lovely," said Susano-wo, his chin resting in his hand.

"Will you help us gain audience with the Judge of the Dead?"

"Hmmm. An interesting challenge," said Susano-wo. "Lord Emma-o, you know, is extremely busy and does not take kindly to being disturbed." The god looked sidelong at me. "You have told her of the danger, haven't you?"

"Danger?" I asked.

"Um," said Goranu.

"The living are forbidden to enter the Court of Lord Emma-o. This is only reasonable, you understand. Think of the chaos it would cause if every family could petition him for the return of their sons, and so forth."

"I have no wish to cause trouble or trespass where I should not," I said. "Could you be so kind as to speak to Lord Emma-o on our behalf?"

Goranu looked scandalized. Susano-wo merely chuckled. "A sensible question, child. I would do it for you gladly — but, you see, my brother and sister gods do not entirely trust me. That is why I am forced to live underground. If I visit Lord Emma-o by myself, he will pay no attention to me and have me thrown out. The two of you might catch his attention long enough to learn something useful."

"Goranu," I said, "is this wise?"

The tengu looked at the ground. "It is the fastest way. We cannot search every heaven and hell for your sister's soul. If you want an answer soon enough to save her, we must take this chance."

"I see."

"Do not be disheartened," said Susano-wo. "I will give what help I can. After all, you are my kinsman, Goranu, loath as I am to admit it. But mostly I will do it to help this charming and clever mortal who has so entertained me with her story."

I blushed and hid my face behind my sleeves.

"Innumerable thanks, O Bringer of Life-Giving Rain!"

"I . . . I also thank you, Great One," I said, prostrating myself beside Goranu.

"It is nothing," said the Storm God, leaping to his feet. "But first some preparations must be made. Come with me, child." He extended his hand to me.

I placed my hand in his and he led me to a brazier beside his drums. It was the fire in this brazier that had lit the cave. Susano-wo reached into the flames with no fear or pain. Indeed, he was not burned at all as he pulled out a handful of ashes.

"You must wear this so that you will be disguised as one of the dead. Hold still. And put down your sleeves. This is no time for modesty."

Feeling foolish, I lowered my arms from my face. He smeared the ashes on my cheeks and forehead with gentle strokes, as if his fingers were ink brushes.

"There," Susano-wo said at last, and stepped back. "Finished. Now I must tell you one more thing. You must not speak while we are in Lord Emma-o's chamber, for your voice will betray you as one of the living. You understand?"

I nodded. What would I possibly say to the Judge of the Dead?

"Good. Now where is—ah, here comes Goranu!"

Goranu came hobbling up to us, one of his legs now a bird's leg and one an old man's. He seemed to be having trouble with his arms, and his nose was longer.

"Don't be so fearful," Susano-wo said to him. "A tengu is safer in hell than in heaven."

"Fearful? Me?" squeaked Goranu. "My Lord, remember you made the tengu as courageous as the hawk that guards its nest."

"Heh. I wish I had made them as noble. I suppose I'd better carry you both. That way we will get there quicker."

Susano-wo picked us up, one under each arm, and he began to run. Down one cavern passage and into another he ran, faster and faster, until the passing of the walls was a blur and I lost all track of how far we had gone. Faster and faster he went, until the pounding of his feet sounded like the thunder of the sacred drums at Ise. The sight of the cave rushing by made me feel ill and I covered my eyes.

I do not know how long he ran with us pressed tight against his sides. Presently the Storm God slowed his pace. Then he stopped and set us down. "We are there," he said softly.

I stood and looked around. We were in an enormous chamber whose walls I could not see for all the gray-faced people who filled it. They were in all manner of dress: high noblemen in black robes and caps, lower functionaries in green, common folk in single-layer kimonos, and the destitute in rags or nothing. They did not seem to note us, but all their gazes were fixed on what was just ahead.

There, on a dais made of wood that glowed with fire, was Lord Emma-o. He was the same size as Susano-wo, but dressed in the black robe and stiff silk hat of a high official. Beneath his fine brows, his eyes glowed like smoldering coals. He seemed to flicker like a flame himself, one moment there, the next moment not.

"This is not his only court," whispered Susano-wo to me. "He has many places he must do his work and can be at each in the blinking of an eye."

Before the Judge was a book, and his hand was a constant blur as it wrote in name after name. He would, on occasion, point at some soul standing in the chamber. That personage would then, with a mournful cry, go flying like an arrow from a bow through one of the many cavernous holes in the wall

behind the Judge. Demons with the heads of horses surrounded the dais, keeping a watchful eye on the throng.

"Greetings, Lord Magistrate!" said Susano-wo.

"So, Susano-wo," said Lord Emma-o, without looking up.
The Judge's voice was like a tremor in the soul, and I shook
with fear and awe.

"I understand you are very busy," the Storm God said.

"Very. Your beloved earthquakes are keeping me so. I had
intended to send a messenger to ask you to cease for a time.
I thank you for saving me the trouble."

"No gratitude is necessary," said Susano-wo. "I bring a
kinsman who would ask a question of you."

"I have no time to answer idle questions."

"O Wise and Learned Judge," said Goranu. "A terrible
thing may have happened—your law may have been sub-
verted!"

The writing brush stopped. Silence filled the chamber.
Lord Emma-o turned his baleful gaze to the tengu. "How is
this so? Be brief."

"The soul of one who has died has stolen the soul of one
who lives. We seek the one to find the other."

I was stung by Goranu's falsehood, but I said nothing.

"Who is the thief?"

"Er . . . Koga no Yugiri, Lord Magistrate. If you can tell
us where you sent him, we can recover the one he stole."

I clenched my fists. It was unjust to accuse Yugiri so, yet
I still did not speak.

Lord Emma-o raised his hand, and the sheets of paper
before him riffled back and forth a few moments. "I see no
record of such a one."

"P-please try to recall him, my Lord Magistrate," said

Goranu. "He is a cousin of the Emperor and he died on the West Road, some ri from the capital. The soul he has stolen is that of the beautiful and accomplished Fujiwara no Amaiko."

With a sigh like the wind from a storm, Lord Emma-o said, "How long ago?"

"Er"—Goranu looked at me, but I could only stare help-lessly back—"um, about a month . . . give or take a few weeks."

Lord Emma-o scowled at Goranu. He gestured at two of the horse-headed demons guarding the dais. These pulled out stacks of folded paper from a chest of drawers behind the magistrate and began to flip through, faster than the eye could watch. The crowd of gray souls around us became rest-less and they glared at us.

After many heartbeats, the demons chittered at one an-other. Then they came forward and flipped through the book just in front of the Magistrate. At last they returned to their posts, shaking their horrible heads.

"He has not come before me," said Lord Emma-o.

"That is impossible," I whispered.

All eyes in the chamber turned to look at me. I realized my error with a sinking of my heart, though I thought no one could have possibly heard me. The gray souls near me shrank back, as if I were diseased. Lord Emma-o's gaze burned into me.

"Who dares trespass in the Realm of the Dead?"

"I told you not to speak!" Susano-wo whispered harshly. I could not move for fear. Goranu jumped between me and the nearest demons.

"P-please, Lord Magistrate," said Goranu. "She meant

no offense. It is on behalf of her and her family that I petitioned you. Let us go in peace and we will trouble you no further."

"Arrest her!"

The guardian demons rushed toward me. Susano-wo pulled a drum mallet from his loincloth and held it up before the demons. They paused and eyed the mallet fearfully.

"Run!" Susano-wo shouted.

I looked wildly around, wondering where we could possibly run to.

"Get on my back!" Goranu said.

I clambered on and Goranu ran for the nearest side passage. Behind us, I could hear the thunder of Susano-wo's mallet and Lord Emma-o's shouts of "How dare you disrupt my proceedings!"

The cave passage was dimly lit. As we ran, taking one turn after another, it seemed that this area was a knotted labyrinth of caves, all entirely similar. I had no idea how we would find a way out.

"Let's try this one," said Goranu, and he hopped sideways through an opening in the wall. "Yaaaah!" he cried.

I screamed as we found ourselves falling down a gigantic pit.

Goranu spread his wings, which stopped our descent. Colorful objects went plummeting past us. After a moment, I could see that they were men and women, whose garments fluttered around them. Like doomed butterflies they fell and fell, shrieking as they went. I was terribly afraid one would land on top of us.

"This must be the Hell of Headlong Falling," said

Goranu. "It is the place where those of loose morality are sent."

"How do we get out of here?"

"I'm not sure. Let me ask someone." Goranu spiraled down until we saw a gentleman falling more slowly than the rest. He had spread out his arms so that his wide sleeves caught the air. He seemed calm and relaxed, as if lying on cushions of wind. Goranu matched speed with him and said, "Good day, Kind Sir."

The fellow looked at us with a wry smile. "Good day to you. You must be a demon."

"That I am, indeed, Sir. A tengu, to be precise."

"How fascinating. And the lovely creature on your back—is she a fox spirit?"

"No, not at all. We seem to have blundered in here by mistake. Could you possibly tell us how to get out?"

"If I knew the way out, would I still be here? They say, of course, if you pray very, very hard and chant the sutras for several years running, you might be granted a reprieve."

"We would rather not wait many, many years," said Goranu.

"Well, I understand," said the gentleman. "But if you stay near me, we might find a way."

"How is that?"

He tilted his head toward us with a grin. "I suspect they are going to send me away from here soon. You see, I am enjoying this place too much. That is not what hells are for, you know. But I find it most pleasant to watch the ladies go tumbling past. Their kimonos are blown aside to show their shapely legs and arms. Most pleasant, indeed."

"But if you are sent from this place, won't you just go to a hell that's worse?"

"Most likely," said the gentleman. "But at least it will be somewhere else."

Unable to help myself, I said, "Please pardon me, sir, but have you seen a Koga no Yugiri here?"

The gentleman laughed. "We do not get much chance to ask each other's names in this place. Most of us are thinking too hard about getting to the next life to concern ourselves with the past one. So I have no idea. Although I remember this one lady— Yaaaah!"

Suddenly someone in bright garments fell on top of the gentleman and he lost his balance in the air. They both plummeted away from us headfirst, arms and legs flailing. More fallers followed, shrieking, passing very close by us.

"A fresh batch of sinners must have come in!" said Goranu.

"What if one of them hits us?" I cried. "Can we get out of here?"

"Ah! I see a passage over there. I'll head for it." Ducking and swooping to avoid the descending bodies, Goranu reached a hole in the pit wall. We ducked in like a cliff bird reaching its nest. I slid off Goranu's back and we stumbled down the low tunnel. There were openings in the passage and I glanced into them as we ran past. I glimpsed sad-eyed souls standing in columns of hot steam or seated on red-glowing stones. Some were held down with heavy weights; others were drowning in foul-smelling pools. I prayed that Yugiri was in none of these, for I would not have the courage to enter them.

Eventually we reached a place where our tunnel split into two ways. A wide flat rock stood before the branching passage. I sat upon it to rest. "Where do we go now?" I asked, feeling weary and without hope.

"We find a way home, that's all," Goranu said grumpily. "With luck, Susano-wo will find us and lead us out again."

"But what about Yugiri?"

"What about him?" snapped Goranu.

"We should keep searching for him, neh?"

Goranu glared down his beak at me. "Do you have any idea how many hells there are? They are as innumerable as the sins of mankind! We could search for twenty lifetimes and not visit them all."

"Oh."

"Besides, Lord Emma-o sees everyone before they are sent where they belong. Lord Emma-o hasn't seen Yugiri. There-fore, to search any more would be futile . . . You'd better not have been lying to me, Little Puddle. We tengu get very peev-ish when tricked. Your family would regret it for generations to come."

"Lying? I have not lied to you, Goranu! You have seen Amaiko. You have seen that her soul is not with her. May the Amida take me and fling me into one of these hells if I have been lying. I swear to you, Goranu! I saw—" I burst into tears, unable to continue.

Goranu patted me with his wing. "So, so—I did not mean to make you cry. Forgive me. I believe you. Stop that, now. I'm just confused as to how your Yugiri could be dead, but the Judge of the Dead not know it."

"I have heard," I said between sobs, "that the blessed can

be taken directly to Amida's Paradise. The very blessed may have a heaven of their own made just for them."

"What would I know of the Amida's Paradise?"

"In fact," I went on, "I do not think Yugiri would be in any hell at all. He was a good man."

"Was he a monk?"

"No, but—"

"Did he chant the sutras every day? Or copy them out in his own hand ninety-nine times?"

"I do not know . . . I have not heard of it."

"Then he probably hasn't been taken into Paradise. Look, I know monks. I know what those silly men go through. From the sound of it, this Yugiri has done nothing monklike."

I sighed, not knowing how to argue with Goranu any further. From the distance came a howl that made my skin prickle.

"They have caught our scent," Goranu whispered.

"Who?"

"Lord Emma-o's demons. Have you forgotten? They have not forgotten us. We'd better run!"

"I am so tired. I do not think I can run anymore."

"How can you complain? *I've* been doing the running for both of us! Here, give me your outermost robe."

"What?"

"Just give it to me. Quickly!"

The howls were coming closer. I was confused but slipped off my outer kimono for him. It had been my second-best overrobe, a figured silk in red shading to green. I helped Goranu put it over his wings.

"Now, you run down that way. I will lead them down this way. Go!"

I hurried down the leftward shaft and went around a sharp bend, while Goranu waited at the fork. I heard him say, in imitation of my voice, "Oh, I am so tired. Whatever shall I do— Eeeeek!"

"There she is!" cried one of the demons. "Snatch her!"

I huddled against the rock wall as I heard many footsteps running down the other passage. Their howls became fainter and fainter. After some moments, there was silence. I waited but heard no other sound. I felt very much alone.

I began to stumble down the passage in which I'd hidden. I no longer cared where it led. It was very brave of Goranu to make the demons chase him instead of me. I wondered if they would hurt him. I imagined Goranu being torn apart by them, and tears came to my eyes. *How surprising that I should weep for a tengu,* I thought. I did not wonder what would become of me. It hardly seemed to matter.

I heard a snuffling noise around the bend behind me. "Perhaps we should look down this way," said a gruff, inhuman voice. "They may have tricked us."

My heart stopped. I was at the entrance to a larger chamber in which pointed, shining columns of stone reached up from the floor and down from the ceiling. Before I could choose where to hide, I heard heavy footsteps approaching from behind.

"Pssst . . . Lady Mitsuko," whispered a feminine voice, "if you please, over this way."

"Where?" I asked, breathless with fear.

"Here." A glowing light appeared between two of the pillars of stone to my left. I stumbled toward the light and slipped between the pillars into a narrow passage. There stood a beautiful noblewoman, a lantern in her hand. She wore the most exquisite gown; it was white at the shoulders, shading to lavender on the sleeves and middle, shading at last to a soft brown at the hem. Her hair was in an elaborate knot held by silver pins.

I bowed low to her. "I thank you—" I began.

There were voices in the chamber behind us. "What's that light? Do you think she went that way?"

The lady touched my arm. "We have no time for such formality, Mitsuko-san. Come."

I let her guide me through another portal. She gestured at a boulder and it rolled with a thunderous rumble, closing off the entrance.

In my amazement, I asked, "Will that stop them?"

The Lady smiled. "They would not dare enter."

I bowed again. "May I know to whom I am in debt for my rescue?"

"I am known in my family as Princess Meiyo."

"Are you, then, of the Emperor's family?"

She laughed. "I do not think so, no."

"What kingdom are you from? China?"

"No, here. This is where I live." She raised her lantern. Before us was an arched bridge of the same pale, glistening stone as the pillars in the room behind us. Beneath the bridge a stream flowed between banks of smooth, rounded rock.

Princess Meiyo led me over the bridge and raised her lantern higher. I gasped at what I saw.

It was a perfect garden, all in stone. The stream meandered past small "bushes" whose white flowers were made of the most delicate crystals. Stone pines nearly touched the high ceiling. Here and there were dimpled rocks of an orange hue, like sprays of chrysanthemums forever in bloom. On one wall of the chamber, stone seemed to flow down to the stream, an eternal frozen waterfall. At the proper places, stone benches rose from the chamber floor; there one could sit and admire the garden. The Princess led me to one of these and we sat.

"How beautiful!" I said.

"It pleases me that you think so. I've often wondered how it would look to others."

"Do you live here all alone?"

"Oh, no. I have many visitors. But they are not here. They are up above."

I was not sure what this meant, but I did not wish to seem rude by questioning her. I sat and admired and wondered, *What sort of poems would Amaiko have written here?* It was quite beyond my skill to describe. What an elegant conversation Amaiko and the Princess might have had! I wished I could overhear it. I, myself, felt as speechless as the stones around me. *Even Goranu would have produced some clever chatter,* I thought. *He should be here to see this, too* . . . And then I remembered.

"You are frowning, Mitsuko-san. What is the matter?"

"I was thinking of my friend Goranu. I fear he is in danger. The demons were chasing him, too."

Princess Meiyo raised her head and her gaze became distant. She said, "The demons have caught him, but they have not yet harmed him."

I could not tell by what skill she knew this, but I did not doubt her sight. "Oh, I hope they do not. He is only a tengu but he has been kind and brave in helping me."

"I will see what I can do." The Princess covered her forehead with her hand. Then, after a moment, she said, "They will leave him alone now."

"You have power over Lord Emma-o's demons?"

She shrugged a little. "Only the power that one who owns a house has over those who live in it. One can request that they not ruin the property."

"Ah." Again I was baffled but chose not to say so.

"If I may be so forward as to ask, Mitsuko-san, what brings you so far from home in the company of a tengu?"

I sighed. I had told my story to so many people that I had wearied of it myself. I said only, "I am searching for the soul of my sister's husband."

"Ah," she said, as if I had explained everything. "Lord Emma-o could not help you?"

"He said he had not seen Yugiri. But that is impossible, if he sees everyone who dies. I thought, perhaps, Yugiri might have been taken into Paradise, but Goranu said that only happens to monks. I am truly perplexed and do not know what to think."

"With all the respect due to them, your friend Goranu and Lord Emma-o do not know everything. This world is wide and strange and many inexplicable things happen."

"So I am learning. Your Highness, you seem so very wise. Could you tell me how I might go about my search?"

Princess Meiyo laughed gently. "Alas, I am not so wise as you hope. I hear the voices of the living, not the dead. But I know of a place where you may find help. I can open a path for you to go there."

"Is it a dangerous place?"

"Oh, no. You will find it quite pleasant, I think."

"Can Goranu come, too?"

"No. I am afraid he must discover his own way. But I can tell him where he might find you later, if you wish."

"That would be very kind of you."

"Then it is done. If you will do me the honor of following me . . ." She took my hand and stood.

The Princess led me out of the garden of stone. We entered into a small, round chamber.

"There is no other way out of here," I said, confused.

Princess Meiyo smiled and lifted her lantern. "Look up."

The chamber had no ceiling—the walls rose in a vertical shaft, disappearing into the darkness above us.

"Where are we?"

"We are near the heart of my mountain. But we will be rising to its summit. Please take hold of my hand."

I placed my hand in hers, wondering who she might truly be. Could she be a bodhisattva, or the avatar of some powerful kami? I began to wish adventuring was not so complicated.

The Princess turned her gaze upward and we began to rise. This was much more disconcerting than flying on Goranu's back. I saw no means by which we were accomplishing it. But I held very still and did not look down. The Princess seemed to regard this manner of movement as ordinary, as if she were merely ascending the steps of a temple.

Up and up we rose, the walls of the shaft never changing. At last, at Princess Meiyo's guidance, I stepped out into a thick mist. There was a faint smell of rotten eggs. I feared I might have been led into a different hell.

"Do not be afraid," said Princess Meiyo. "You wished to learn of your sister's husband's fate. I will send you to those who can assist you."

"Forgive me, but why are you doing this kindness for me?"

The Princess blinked. "Because you called to me. You prayed for my assistance from far out there, and I have been waiting for the chance to answer you."

I covered my mouth with my sleeves then, for it had fallen open in a most unsightly manner. I bowed deeply, for she could be no other than an avatar of Fuji-sama herself. When I looked up again, she held several sticks of incense in her hand.

"Most High and Glorious Lady-Mountain, where is it you are sending me?"

"To the one place where the fate of souls is everyone's business—to the Land of the Ancestors. I cannot tell you what you will see there, but a relative of yours will come to greet you." With the tip of her finger, she lit five of the sticks of incense and placed them in a hole in a nearby boulder. The scent they released was indescribable, yet it awakened in me thoughts of my favorite flowers, in my favorite garden, in the best of seasons. My fondest memories lingered just out of reach of my thoughts. Surely if anything could bind my soul to this world of illusion and sorrows, such a perfume could.

"This is the Incense of Souls' Recall."

"Ah. If only . . . Highness, if you could possibly—"

"Do not ask, Mitsuko-san. You could not use this yourself to bring your sister's husband back. That is not its power.

But so long as these burn, you may stay in the Land of the Ancestors. Once they are exhausted, you will return to this world."

"I do not know how I will ever repay your kindness."

"That you have thought of me and included me in your prayers is gratitude enough. Please be on your way, before you lose much time." She raised her arm and I followed the direction of her gesture. With a final bow to Princess Meiyo, I stepped into the mist.

Little Sister of Smoke

O fortunate smoke,
you rise heavenward with ease,
but I am earthbound.

*W*HEN THE MIST parted before me, I was standing in
a garden. It was a very ordinary garden. Purple iris bloomed
along one edge of the path on which I stood. A dwarf maple
on the path's other side bore colorful autumn leaves. Carefully tended and shaped pines stood here and there among
moss- and fern-covered hillocks. Between them ran a little
stream, its flow broken only by a line of round stepping-
stones. It was not at all as wondrous as the cave garden of
Princess Meiyo, but I felt instantly at peace; almost . . . at
home.

I walked along the path until I saw a house. It was not a

large house, yet it was so well kept it could have been the retreat of a refined noble family. I stopped, wondering how I should announce myself. It seemed improper to simply walk in.

To my left, I noticed some sheets of mitchoku paper held beneath a rock. A brush and inkstone lay beside them. Apparently someone had been planning to write or had just done so. To give myself time to think, I sat beside the stream. Taking one sheet of paper, I wetted the brush and rubbed it against the inkstone. For practice, I wrote this poem:

> *How far through many*
> *lands I've walked, only to*
> *find myself at home.*

When I looked up, I was surprised to see a little serving girl standing beside me. Her hair was cut at shoulder length, and she wore a very becoming, simple kimono of white shading to crimson. She smiled at me but said nothing. I did not know what to say. For some reason I could not name, I folded the paper I had written my poem on around a fallen leaf and handed it to her.

She bowed and trotted to the house. I stood, unsure if I should follow her. In a few moments, she came out of the house again, followed by an old woman.

"Mitsuko!" the elderly lady cried with a grin. "Mitsu-chan, you've come to visit us!"

"Obaa-san!" I said, my heart leaping. My grandmother had died when I was eight years old, and yet here she was again, just as I remembered her. We clasped hands with tears in our eyes, and Grandmother shook with joy.

"What a gift!" she said. "Some children just put out
at O-Bon, but you come yourself to visit! Come in! C
in! There are so many here who will want to see you!"

I let her lead me into the tidy house, and we sat o
cushions as servants came from nowhere bearing tea an
cakes. I noticed there were faces peering around the
sliding doors. Grandmother turned to them and said
all right. She will not bite you. Come in and meet Mi

And person after person, male and female, young,
aged, and old, filed in to fill the room. They all smi
bowed to me as Obaa-san introduced each one
cousin, uncle, great-aunt, or great-great-grandfathei
on. They sat and stared at me hungrily, as if there w
ing more they ached for than some news, some coi
the living world.

"So, tell us," said Obaa-san to me, "tell us ever
has been happening with you."

"It is not good news," I said, "and I have lii
which to speak. I am here by the kindness and s
cess Meiyo, and I cannot outstay my time."

There was much *tsk*ing and *tut*ting and groa
the relatives at this.

As briefly as I could, I told them of Amai
and our flight from Heian Kyō and the terribl
had befallen us. Many in the room were we
finished. "I have come here," I said at last,
Yugiri's soul, for I fear Amaiko has followed h

"Well!" said Grandmother, getting up, be
easily answered. Come with me."

I stood and took Obaa-san's arm. The re ng

the room cleared a path for us and we walked out to a different veranda than the one facing the garden. I gasped when I beheld the view.

There was another house across a gap, standing on huge bamboo stilts. Below it was another house contained within he same bamboo structure. To either side of me, as far as I ould see, stood houses side by side, connected by bridges or dders or ropes. I knelt down on the veranda and peered er the edge. It was houses all the way down.

"This is the Land of the Ancestors," said Obaa-san. very family has their home, but of course they are all inconnected. I have heard it said that if one travels down far ugh, one will reach the First Pair, Izanagi and Izan--but that may be simply an old soul's tale. This way, u-chan."

followed her along the veranda until we came to a beau- little bridge. It had been built and painted recently, and ing cords only slightly weathered still adorned its posts. appeared at your sister's marriage," said Obaa-san. With y sigh, she added, "I am sorry it will not get much use

elt tears filling my eyes and I could not reply. In silence lked slowly across the bridge. Again the serving girl ed out of nowhere and followed us. The building at er end of the bridge had large hardwood beams and nboo blinds. It appeared to be a minor wing of the r's Palace. The serving girl ran ahead and disappeared wall of the mansion. She returned again shortly led us up onto the broad veranda, where cushions ıs.

We sat on these, and presently someone sat on the other side of the bamboo blinds. From the perfume wafting out to our noses and the fine sleeve hems that draped out from beneath the blinds, I could tell a very well-born Lady now graced us with her company.

"I am told you are searching for Koga no Yugiri," she said in a low voice.

"It is so," said Obaa-san. "Thank you for your kindness in giving us assistance."

"It is no trouble to me, save that your visit troubles me."

"We are so sorry to be the bearers of sad news."

"I am not sure what sort of news you bring. I do not understand why you would seek him here. But it does not matter. I have not seen Yugiri. He has not come to this land."

"Are you sure?" I asked. It was terribly rude, but I could not stop myself.

"I am very certain," said the Lady, somewhat coldly, "for I am his mother. I died when Yugiri was a child. Had he come to this land, I would have been the first to greet him."

"Forgive me," I said softly. "I did not know."

"I understand. You are in haste and could not take the time to learn what is proper here."

"As Mitsuko is not yet of our world," said Obaa-san, "there is much she cannot know of us. For example, that we can, at times, see our living relations as the living sometimes see us — in dreams, or in night shadows, or in the reflections of water. Perhaps if you have had such visions of your son, you may more precisely correct Mitsuko's error."

"Believe me, I would do so, were it possible. But the visions I have had of Yugiri have been . . . clouded . . .

shadowed. It is as if he does not wish us to see him. Or something interferes . . ." Her voice trailed off sadly.

I did not know what this might mean, so I said nothing.

As if to encourage me, Obaa-san said, "And yet, Mitsu-chan, you have told us that you saw Yugiri fall."

"I saw our servants carry his body away. They would not let me look at him, for the uncleanliness it would have brought upon me."

"Under what circumstances did his . . . falling occur?" asked the Lady.

"He was defending us from thieves."

"Hm. That is noble, but not uplifting. Did he pass away with the words of a sutra upon his lips?"

"Lady, I do not know. I and my sisters were praying for him, though."

"The prayers of children would scarcely be of use to him, I think. But it is possible that he paid some monk or other to copy the sutras for him, in which case he may have earned himself a place on Mount Tai or the Heaven of Golden Peak, or some other paradise we know nothing of."

"However would I find him then?" Despair crept upon me.

"You must go to a great temple," the Lady said, as if explaining to me the simplest poem, "and pray for a vision. Now, I beg your forgiveness, but I have other business to attend to. Good fortune to you, Child of the Fujiwara. Should you find my son, tell him to send word to me."

"I will do so," I said, bowing. I heard the rustle of her kimonos as she departed, though the perfume she left behind seemed to have become sour.

As Obaa-san and I crossed back over the bridge, she said, "Well! That one certainly received us at the end of her nose, neh?"

"I suppose she is unhappy about Yugiri."

"You are a good and kind child, Mitsu-chan. May you never lose such qualities."

As we reached the center of the bridge, I scented a familiar smell . . . It was the Incense of Souls' Return. On the other side of the bridge, all my relatives were gathered. But they began to fade, even as I watched.

"I must go now!" I called out to them. "Good-bye! Fare you well!"

"Good-bye!" they all shouted back. "How good it was to see you! We will miss you!"

I realized I would miss them also. How true is the saying that to be far from family is the greatest poverty.

Obaa-san turned to me and said, "I hope someday we may be together again . . . but not too soon, neh?"

"Remember us!" the relatives called, just before they all faded and a mist surrounded me.

The mist smelled of incense and woodsmoke — like a funeral pyre. I coughed, and as the smoke cleared, I found myself in a forest of burial stones . . . or a graveyard. I looked around for a funeral procession but saw no one. I was alone.

As carefully as I could, I stepped around the stones, softly whispering the Lotus Sutra to hold off baleful spirits. Then I stopped. I could hear, close ahead of me, someone sniffling and weeping.

I peered around a gravestone and saw a young man with

a long nose, dressed in a black robe. He was going from marker to marker, reading them, searching for something. He seemed truly pathetic as he mumbled to himself between sobs. I stepped out from behind the stone. "Please, Sir, you seem so very sad. Is there any way I may help you?"

He looked up at me. And then he jumped up, shrieking, "Little Puddle! Little Puddle—it is you!" He danced and flapped his arms and made motions as if to touch me, but I stepped back.

"Goranu?"

"Of course I am Goranu! Are you . . . are you alive?"

"I think so." I pinched myself and felt flesh between my fingers. "How is it you are here?"

"It was a strange thing," said the tengu. "The demons of Lord Emma-o had caught me and they were going to beat me for my trickery. Then, suddenly, they left off and went away. A beautiful Lady in a purple kimono appeared and told me a riddle. She said I would find you in the place between the mortal world and the Land of the Ancestors. I found my Esteemed Ancestor Susano-wo and asked him where such a place might be. He laughed and picked me up and dumped me here. I thought you were dead!"

"Oh, of course! Princess Meiyo promised me she would help you find me."

"Princess Meiyo?" Goranu said, wide-eyed.

"Yes. She rescued me from the demons. And she showed me her beautiful cave garden. And she burned for me the Incense of Souls' Recall so that I might visit the Land of the Ancestors."

"The Lady Fuji? She did all this for you? Why?"

I looked shyly at the ground. "I had prayed to her and asked for her help."

"Hmp. She must have recognized that you are special because you are graced with the company of a tengu. All kami know that we have excellent taste in companions."

"It must be so," I said, for I did not wish to hurt his pride.

"So! What did you learn in the Land of the Ancestors?"

"I saw my grandmother and many of my family."

"Yes, yes, but what of Yugiri? Was he there?"

"No. I spoke to his mother and she had not seen him either. Not even in her dreams."

Goranu sighed and slapped his arms against his sides. "So. I guess there is nothing we can do to solve this mystery."

"Yugiri's mother suggested I visit a great temple and pray for a vision."

"Gnrrrr," said Goranu. "Temple. Priests. Monks. You know what little use they are."

"But—" I heard snuffling again, not far away. *Another mourner?* I thought, turning my head toward the sound. Then I heard a low, gruff voice.

"I smell her. She is here."

I backed into Goranu and he grabbed my shoulders. "It is Lord Emma-o's demons!" I gasped.

"Of course," Goranu said. "This is a burial ground, and thus his domain. Of course he can find you here. We must leave quickly!"

Tugging me by my sleeve, Goranu led me through a bewildering labyrinth of tomb markers. I felt dizzy and despaired of evading the demons again. But Goranu found the

gate and we ran out. We did not dare look back but continued running down a winding path.

Suddenly our way was blocked by a line of people walking up a hill. Not knowing what else to do, we joined the
line, hoping to hide ourselves within it.

After a few moments it became apparent the demons were
not following us. But we were trapped in the throng of people
around us, and we had no choice but to move along with
them. They were praying and chanting, some running beads
through their hands. *These are pilgrims,* I realized.

"Excuse me, if you please, Esteemed Sir," I said to a man
beside me, "where are we going?"

The gentleman looked at me with a bemused smile. He
was perhaps of fifty years and dressed in well-made robes of
gray. "Good afternoon to you, Neighbor!" he said. He had
the pleasant countenance of one who has laughed often in
his life. "How can you not know?"

"We are here quite by accident," I said.

He raised his brows. "Are you so sure? Do you never feel
that divine hands guide you to a certain place or action?
Perhaps it is no accident that you are here at all."

"That may well be true, Sir," I said.

"As it happens, this procession is going to the Temple of
Kiyomizudera. They are consecrating a new bell there
today."

"How amazing!" I said. "Someone has told me I should
seek out a temple and pray for a vision."

"You see?" said the gentleman. "It is all for a purpose.
Forgive me, but your servant seems ill."

"Gnrrrr," said Goranu.

"He ... has come a very long way," I temporized. "Goranu?" I whispered to the tengu. He only plodded along, staring at the ground.

"I beg your pardon for my nosiness," said the gentleman, "but aren't you a very young lady to come so far on foot with only one servant?"

"Her family has been through difficult circumstances," growled Goranu.

"Ah, a great pity. Please forgive me," said the pilgrim. "You have come to pray for your family, then, neh?"

"Yes," I said, "for my sister and her husband."

"I am sure such an earnest young lady as you are will find her prayers granted. Ah, we are nearly there."

I looked up and saw we had reached a stairway set into a hillside. The procession was packed very tightly, as the pilgrims had squeezed onto the narrow steps. Halfway up the hill was the temple gate and near the top of the hill was perched the temple itself. Beside the temple stood a platform, above which hung an enormous bronze bell. Two monks pulled back on a great beam that swung on ropes and let it go. It struck the bell, which rang in such deep tones that I shivered with awe. I knew I had somehow, indeed, been led to the right place.

Goranu moaned and covered his ears.

"Goranu?" I said. And then, with a shock, I understood. *He is a demon. It will harm him to walk on holy ground.* I tried to stop and look around, to see if there were some way he could get out of the throng. But the crush of people pushed us inexorably up the hill, as if we were caught in a slow, inescapable flood.

The pilgrims behind me scowled at us for trying to stop. "Move, if you please, or we will all be trampled!" they said.

"If you are ill, friend," said the gentleman to Goranu, "let us carry you up and we will all pray for your recovery. I understand one of the monks here is an excellent healer."

"N-n-n-o!" said Goranu. He gazed up at the temple with wide, fearful eyes.

We were pushed closer and closer to the gate. Goranu began to grimace.

"Goranu, I must go in, but do not follow me if it hurts you. Wait for me and I will look for you when I am done."

Shaking, Goranu reached into his sleeve and pulled out a big black feather. He gave it to me and said, "If you hold this and call for me, I will come to you no matter where you are. But only use it if you truly need me."

"I will. You should go now," I said, though I did not see how he could, so closely were we hemmed in on all sides.

"There is nothing to fear, Friend," said the pilgrim. "I will start a chant for you to soothe your soul." He began to recite the first stanza of the Golden Sutra.

Goranu screamed and jumped into the air. With a loud bang, just above our heads he turned into a bird. He flew low over the amazed pilgrims on the stairs. Then he disappeared into a pine grove far down the hill.

"How astonishing!" said the pilgrim. "Your servant is a tengu! I've only heard about them in stories. I never thought I would see one until now!"

"Um," I said, feeling abandoned and somewhat sad.

"No wonder he wouldn't go into the temple."

"It would have hurt him, neh?"

"Oh, more than that. If a tengu should actually accept the True Path and the Holy Teachings, he would die."

"Ah." What a dilemma. I thought of Goranu as a friend, and does not everyone want a friend to find the True Path? And yet, and yet—not at the price of his life.

I clutched his feather tightly as I entered the temple gate.

As we filed into the temple, the pilgrim, to my annoyance, kept pointing me out to whatever monks we passed. "She was in the company of a tengu!" he said.

So when I finally reached the women's area, two monks came to me and asked, "Are you the one seen with the tengu?"

I disliked the attention, but speaking falsehood in that holy place would have been worse. "Yes, so it would seem."

"Come with us." And I was led directly to the feet of the Sacred Image.

This clearly upset some of the higher-ranked lady pilgrims. But I was given no chance to offer apologies. The monks placed before me a little incense burner with sandalwood in it.

"Pray well," counseled the monks. "Pray that your soul has not been tainted by the demon's wickedness."

I felt confused. Goranu may have been impious, but he did not seem in any way wicked. The monks hurried off and I was left to my prayers. While shifting my gowns for comfort, I noticed something in my left sleeve. I reached in and pulled out a piece of rice cake from the Land of the Ancestors. I placed this on the incense burner as an offering—it was all I had to give.

The smoke from the censer made me drowsy, and after I

mumbled the first twenty-one stanzas of the Lotus Sutra, I must have nodded off.

Someone shook my shoulder and I looked up. A young monk was earnestly staring down at me. He had taken a great liberty to touch me so, but I did not speak. "I have been told your story and it is most extraordinary," said the monk. "I think you had better come with me."

I did not know what to do. So many monks nowadays did not behave according to their strictures. I looked around the room, but it was now empty.

"This way, Lady, if you please," said the young monk. "No one will harm you."

I followed, feeling I had no choice. To my astonishment, he led me to the innermost garden of the temple. Usually such a place is considered very holy and only the temple monks themselves can enter it. I covered my face with my sleeves and gazed around, but I saw no one else.

I saw little of the garden, for that matter, for a heavy fog had drifted down the mountainside.

I followed the monk along a narrow path that wound between pine trees. Their boughs reached out of the mist as if to catch me.

The monk stopped at a wooden staircase that led steeply up the slope. He stepped aside and held out his arm toward the stairs. "This is the way you ought to go, Lady," he said.

I sighed, for the steps seemed very steep. But I did not want to stay in the mysterious sanctuary. I pulled up the hems of my kimonos and began to climb the stairs. I did not count how many steps there were. I only remember that just as I thought I could bear no more, I reached the top.

Before me was a clearing surrounded by boulders. The fog lurked just beyond the rocks, but it was thinner and seemed illuminated by some light beyond or within it. A lone tree grew in the center of the clearing. Beneath it, a young man sat cross-legged, eyes shut in meditation. He wore only a loincloth.

I took a couple of steps toward him and then sank to my knees in exhaustion. "Forgive me for intruding upon your tranquility," I said to him. "But can you tell me where I am and why I have been sent here?"

The young man did not answer. Indeed, he did not even open his eyes.

I crept a little closer, thinking he had not heard me. "Please pardon me," I said a little louder, "but could you kindly tell me where I am?"

Again there came no response. I wondered if he had lost his hearing. Or perhaps his meditation was so deep that he truly had fled this world of illusion. I reached out with one finger and gently touched his shoulder. His flesh was warm, but again he showed no sign of knowing I was there. I confess I was somewhat fascinated. I dropped one rock against another with a loud *clack*. He did not even flinch. I picked up a fallen branch from the tree and shook it in front of his face, making the leaves hiss and rattle. Nothing. I sat back, amazed. I reached the branch to his face and tickled his nose, expecting he might at least sneeze. But, again, nothing.

I sighed, as I was tiring of this game. And I was beginning to worry, for I had no idea where I was. I said, "Please, Kind Sir, in the name of merciful Kannon, please speak to me."

He was still as a statue.

Exasperated, I dropped the branch onto the young man's leg with a *thwack*.

"Ai!" he said, his eyes opening.

"A thousand pardons I beg," I said, bowing deeply. "I did not mean to hurt you. I only wanted your attention."

He rubbed his leg but did not seem angry. "So. Now you have it." He focused his large brown eyes on me.

"Thank you. Um. Could you please tell me where I am?"

"No," said the young man.

"I have given apology for striking you. Please do not be rude."

"I am not being rude. I cannot tell you."

"You do not know either?"

"I cannot tell you in a way you would understand."

"I am not stupid."

He gazed at me with a mixture of pity and amusement. "Intelligence has nothing to do with it. It is what you have learned that matters."

"I am a Fujiwara and my family has educated me well."

He smiled. "Recite for me the Sutra of the Hunter's Bow."

"I . . . I was not taught that one."

"There is no such sutra. Nor could there be. You know less than you think."

"Well, what does that matter? I only want to know where I am."

"Where do you think you are?"

I looked around but gained no further clue from the boulders and the mist. "Somewhere near the Temple of Kiyomizudera."

The young man laughed. "You see? You believe you are in this place, but in fact, this place is within *you.*"

He was right. I did not understand. I thought perhaps he was playing word games with me, so I looked away. "Why did the temple monk tell me to come here?" I said to myself.

"You wanted to be here," said the young man.

I glared at him. "That is foolish. Why should I want to be here?"

"Only you know the answer."

He was hopeless. I sighed and picked up small pebbles from the ground and let them run through my hands.

"Why did you go to the Temple of Kiyomizudera?" he asked.

"I wanted a vision."

"What sort of vision? Was there a question you wanted answered?"

"Of course."

"What is your question?"

I gazed at the ground. What good was it to tell him anything if he was going to play at riddles with me?

"Now it is you who are being rude," he said. "As long as you are here, you might as well tell me."

"I am searching for my sister's husband's soul. I have gone to places you would not believe in this search. But I have not found him. No one I speak to has seen him."

"There is a place you have not looked."

"Clearly! But how am I to know what that place is?"

The young man stood. He seemed larger now. "You must think about all you have learned, Little Puddle, and look into your heart. You will need all your courage to face the truth, for it is a horrible truth you will discover. But once you know it, you have the power to help set matters right."

He knew my name.

"Who are you?" I whispered, looking up at him. He seemed to have grown into the clouds. "Can you not simply tell me what to do?"

"The truth is taken more to heart when discovered by the seeker. It is my place only to set your feet on the Path."

I recognized his face now, from statues I had seen. "Miroku? The Buddha Who Is Yet To Be?"

He was now fading into a layer of multicolored clouds that streamed across the sky. I could see blissful faces in the clouds. He smiled. "Return, Little Puddle. And remember."

The ground beneath me vanished and I was falling. I screamed and took Goranu's feather from my sleeve. "Goranu! Help me! Goranu!" The air rushing past billowed and buffeted my robes.

Then, suddenly, I opened my eyes. I was in the temple prayer room and someone was shaking me.

"Ooch! Ouch! Ooch!" Goranu said beside me. "Aren't you awake yet? We've got to leave! Get up!"

I stood, unsteady, and turned. Goranu, in old man form, was dancing from foot to foot, grimacing in pain. The floor just beneath his feet was glowing red-hot.

"Hurry! I'll have no feet at all if we stay longer!"

I let him grab my sleeve and we ran through the assembled noblewomen like a pair of foxes among peacocks. They clucked and shrieked and scattered out of our way.

Out on the hillside, Goranu changed into bird form and I jumped onto his back. We flew a short way until we reached a broad river. Goranu landed, planting his feet in the shallow water at the river's edge. I slid off his back and crawled onto a nearby rock. Goranu made strange growling noises as steam rose from the water around his feet.

I felt dizzy and confused. The odd dialogue with Miroku must have been the vision I had hoped for. But I felt no more enlightened than I was before. I gazed across the river. Not far beyond its other bank was a walled city whose tiled roofs glinted in the afternoon sun. I realized with a shock it could only be Heian Kyō.

"Goranu! I'm home! This river must be the Kamogawa." A little way upstream was Gojo Bridge, where the Tōkkaido road crossed into the capital. The bridge was full of people, yet I felt like a ghost watching them, not a part of their world.

Goranu, now in young man form, stepped out of the river and collapsed on the sandy bank. "So it is, Little Puddle." He sighed. "If you want to go back to your father, I'm sure someone can lead you there. I will try to get word to my village to have your sister sent to you."

I quickly knelt beside him. "Are you all right?"

He pointed at the blackened lumps that were his feet. "You call *that* all right? No, I am not *all right.* I wonder if I'll ever walk again!"

Tears came to my eyes. "I am so sorry. I did not mean for this to happen. Of course a tengu should not enter a temple. I did not want you to be hurt for my sake. I did not know I was still in Kiyomizudera. I was having a vision, and in the vision I was falling and—"

"So, so, it does not matter now," sighed Goranu.

"I don't even care that you cannot accept the True Path

because it would—it would—" I could not continue speaking for the tears running down my face.

"So, so," said Goranu, "I am only a tengu, after all. You need not waste your sorrow on me. I'm sure the priests told you that your soul was damned because you have been around me."

His words only made me weep more. His feet were so burned and cracked and bleeding, they moved me to great pity. I tore the sleeves from my outermost robe. I no longer remember whether it was my fourth- or fifth-favorite kimono—it didn't matter. I carefully wrapped a sleeve around each of his feet.

"What are you doing?"

"I must do something. You have done so much for me." I looked at him, and tears appeared in his eyes as well. "Please come with me to my father's house," I said. "I will not tell him you are a tengu. There you can heal until you are able to return to your village. I will see that no monks come near you. It is the least I can do in gratitude for your help."

"You amaze me," said Goranu, staring at me. "But as I am a tengu and not a fool, I will gladly accept your offer, unlike some who would refuse a woman's help."

This made me very happy and I smiled at him.

"You are very pretty, you know."

"Do not be so forward, silly tengu," I said, "or I will slap your feet."

"Ooch." He winced in imagined pain. "I shall watch my tongue, you may be sure. Now, let me see." He turned his gaze toward Gojo Bridge and narrowed his eyes. "There are a pair of rice farmers on this side of the bridge, leading an oxcart. They are poor but honest men. They are arguing about something and might be there for a while. You must go to them and give them this." He reached into one sleeve and pulled out two small bars of silver. "Give these to the men and ask them to bring their oxcart here. Tell them there will be two more if they agree to transport us, and two more when we reach our destination."

"Where did you get these?" I asked as I took the silver.

He shrugged. "I stole them from the temple. I am a tengu, after all."

I suppose I should have rebuked him, but I could only laugh. I struggled to my feet and ran off to the bridge. There I found the men arguing . . . They seemed to be father and son. I gave them the silver and told them that an injured nobleman needed their oxcart. As the men had been discussing how they would find lodging without trading away their rice, they readily agreed. The older man followed me back to where Goranu lay, and he carried him on his shoulders to the cart.

Thus we rode back into the capital. Riding on a rude oxcart in our tattered robes, we were not at all a grand sight. Yet I felt so pleased to be home again that I wanted to burst into song. I spoke this aloud and the rice farmers sang for us a saibara all about working in the rice fields, and the women planting the little shoots in the mud.

I told them where my father's house was — how it was two blocks west of thus-and-such wing of the Palace. Fortunately, the farmers had been to the capital before and knew where the Palace was. My heart grew lighter as buildings more and more familiar came into view. We turned a corner, and the men shouted, "Here we are! I think . . ."

I hopped off the back of the cart and ran up beside the ox. And stopped.

There was no house there. Only charred wood and ashes. My father's house had burned to the ground.

Little Sister of Metal

Among the ashes,

I find a melted lump.

Is it iron? No, gold!

I STARED AT the pile of charred wood and ashes. I did not want to move. I did not want to speak or hear or see.

I was aware that people were gathering around the rice farmers' cart. I heard their voices but did not try to understand their words. Now I understood how Amaiko could so close herself off from this world. My thoughts were nowhere but among the burned ruins.

Someone came up beside me and shook my shoulder. "Hey. Hey, Mountain Puddle."

I turned. It was Mochi, the rice cake girl. Could she be so cruel as to mock my sorrow to my face?

"Hey, don't be sad. Nobody was in the house when it burned. Nobody died in the fire."

"No one died?" My voice was but a breath of wind.

"No one. Your papa and all the servants left about ten days ago."

"Where did they go?"

Mochi shrugged. "Don't know. Looking for you and your mama and sisters, I suppose."

So many thoughts rushed into my mind then, like birds gathering to peck at the same crumb. Had Papa found Mama and Kiwako and Sōtōko and Yūshō? What would he think upon hearing Amaiko and I had run away? Did any of them miss me? Was Amaiko all right?

"So, then, Little Lady," the older rice farmer called down to me, "all is well. No one is hurt. One of your neighbors will take you in until your papa comes back, neh? Who here is her neighbor?"

"I serve in the house two gates that way," said a thin, officious chamberlain.

"She can come stay with you, then, right?"

"Oh, no, she mustn't," said the chamberlain. "This street will be blocked by the Demon of the Northwest for the next ten days. It would bring very bad fortune for her to come this way. Even I must travel elsewhere to sleep tonight."

The rice farmers looked knowingly at each other. "Ah, these fine folks and their directional demons," said the younger. "How difficult life must be for them."

Goranu sat up in the cart and looked over their shoulders. "And an ugly brute that demon is, too. Best not to go that way, Little Puddle."

I still do not know if Goranu was joking. Perhaps he had truly seen a demon. Or perhaps he was referring to the chamberlain.

"If the puddle would not mind flowing down a lesser street," said Mochi, "she could come and stay at my house."

I did not know how to reply. It would be a scandal to my family if I took hospitality in such a lowly residence. But the crowd was dispersing, offering apologies, saying bad fortune would follow if I came their way, but wishing me well.

"The puddle sees no other channel in which to flow," I said softly.

"Good," said Mochi. "You fellows come, too," she said to the rice farmers. "My father needs rice. You can probably make a sale."

The farmers agreed that this seemed a good idea.

"Will you give us a taste of your rice cakes?" said Goranu.

"Who are you?" said Mochi.

"That is Goranu," I said. "He has been in my service these past few days."

"Why are his feet all bound up like that?"

"I stepped in a cooking hearth," said Goranu. "They are burned and I can't walk."

The rice farmers laughed. "You are supposed to remove the meat from the bones before cooking it."

I was disgusted by this turn of conversation.

"Could you find no smarter servant than that?" Mochi asked.

"You're a fine judge," Goranu called back before I could reply. "No doubt you've pounded your thumb with a rice mallet once or twice."

"Never," said Mochi. "I watched my brother do it and learned from his mistake. I live this way. Come on."

I climbed back into the cart, feeling shamed. How could I have fallen so low as to need the help of the rice cake girl? Yet why should I feel ashamed of the one person who offered me comfort? Did I earn this bad fortune by being in the company of a tengu? Had there been some connection between me and Mochi in a former life? I hid beneath the remnants of my sleeves and hoped no one watched the cart as it passed.

> *So full of fond hope,*
> *the weary traveler comes home*
> *and finds no home there.*
>
> *What emptiness there is*
> *to exist, and yet live nowhere.*

Soon the cart stopped. I could tell, even before looking up, that we were far from the homes of people of quality. The sounds—babies wailing, dogs barking, people yelling at one another in harsh language—these would have been enough. But the smells! Indescribable. I wished I could choose not to breathe.

There was an argument nearby and I realized it must be Mochi and her family, from the sound of their voices. At last they seemed to reach some agreement. I was helped down from the cart by a big, muscular youth whom Mochi introduced as her brother. Mochi guided me into the house. Her brother picked up Goranu and carried the tengu inside on his back.

Such a miserable place it was. Three rooms only; the front area was being used as a shop. The floor was unpolished wood. I was led through a faded cotton curtain into the back room. Here Mochi's mother bowed and greeted me. Her kimono was silk, and I am sure it was the finest she owned, yet I could tell from the dull color and irregular weave that it was very poor quality. I nodded to her and thanked her for her kind hospitality to one in need.

I paid little attention to their flattering patter as Mochi's mother and father hovered around me. They guided me to a corner of the room where they had set up a rough kichō made from some broken piece of furniture with a swath of much mended cloth draped over it. I knelt gratefully behind this curtain of modesty, yet wished it were even more private so that no one might hear me weep.

Goranu was set on some cushions in another corner. He seemed to enjoy the fuss made over him. Mochi's mother brought unguents for his feet, clucking over how lucky he was that the burns were not worse.

Worse? I thought. *What horrid burns has this poor woman seen, that she has seen worse than Goranu's blackened feet?*

Mochi's father went off to talk business with the rice farmers. Mochi herself came behind my kichō with a tray. The girl had much to learn about proper comportment with a lady, but I was so tired and grateful I did not chide her. She poured out a cup of thick green tea. The aroma was wonderful. She uncovered one bowl that held barley soup and another that contained rice cakes, sliced daikon, and carrots. I nibbled and drank a little and felt more alive.

"You've changed," Mochi said.

"How would you know? We've rarely spoken to each other."

Mochi laughed. "You would be surprised at how much we lowly folk see. But now, I think, the mountain puddle has flowed farther than this little sparrow ever flew."

"Yes. Perhaps. I have been on a long pilgrimage."

"Where did you go?"

I paused. "You would never believe me."

Mochi tilted her head. "I'm not stupid."

"That is not what I meant. I would not believe it myself, had I not been to those places and done those things."

"What places? What things?"

I only shook my head.

Mochi sighed and stood. "You stink of the road. I'd better go pour you a bath."

So tired was I that I scarcely moved before Mochi returned, her hair and skin all damp, to guide me to the bath. It was in the alley behind the shop. It was only a small half barrel filled with hot water — the steam still smelled faintly of the plum wine the barrel had once contained. Nonetheless, I gratefully undressed and slid into it. Cloth had been draped over ropes strung around the barrel for my privacy. Now and then I heard Mochi scolding someone, her brother perhaps, for trying to peep at me.

Night had fallen. As I lay in the hot water, I watched the steam rise up to the bright stars. The vapor twisted and danced, like spirits reaching for the heavens but fading before they could hope to touch it. The strange noises of the street became distant to me. My gaze also reached toward the lights in the sky. I wondered if I had a guardian star, as it was said all good people did. "Please tell me, if you are there," I whispered, "where I am to go and what I am to do."

There came no answer, so at last, soggy and wrinkly, I stepped out of the bath. Mochi wrapped me in clean white cloths that had been nearly worn through in places. We went back behind the kichō, where she applied a towel to my hair and tried to brush it.

"Your hair is a mess. It is like a bird's nest!" said Mochi.

"Yes, I imagine so. It has been much in the wind."

"Doesn't your servant take proper care of you?"

"He is a — man. He is not good at brushing hair."

"Why don't you have a lady servant?"

"I did, but — it is a long story."

"Hmp. Well, that fellow is strange."

"Strange?"

"He has a big nose."

A laugh burst out of me. "It is like a beak, neh?" I gasped. I could not help myself, yet I could not say why it was so amusing. Yet Mochi and I fell on each other, laughing until we were out of breath.

"What are you two cackling about?" asked Goranu, from his corner.

"Nothing that servants should hear," said Mochi.

"Servants hear everything," said Goranu. "I suppose next you'll be exclaiming about how skinny my legs are."

This sent us into more peals of giggling, until Mochi's mother came by and called for her. Mochi went out and I heard them softly discussing something. Mochi returned holding a bundle of cloth.

"Mama says that she is washing your inner garments and will repair them tonight if she can. But she says the hems are beyond repair and asks your forgiveness that they cannot be made as new."

"I understand," I said. "Your family's hospitality is most generous. I could not possibly complain."

"She hopes," said Mochi, looking at the floor, "that your family will be generous in turn when you tell them of our kindness."

Bold as always. Was the whole family so? "I will whisper it into my father's ear every day to remind him. When I find him." I sighed.

Mochi unwound the bundle of silk cloth she held. I recognized it—it was the fourth-best kimono that I had given her so long ago. She paused, lightly stroking the fabric. "Mama said I should have traded this for something more useful, but I didn't want to." She held it out to me. "Now I think you need this more than I."

"I could not take my gift back from you. How rude that would be! Please keep it."

Mochi's mouth curled up in a wry smile. "Mama always says that Those Who Live Above the Clouds would do well to be less polite and more sensible. Look." Mochi reached behind her and picked up the outer kimono I had been wearing. It was a ruin. I had torn off the sleeves for Goranu's bandages, of course, but the hem was filthy and frayed and the silk was horribly stained. "You would rather wear *this* again? What would your papa have thought had you shown up on his doorstep in such garments? My mama can take this and pick it apart for rags or make a child's kimono out of it. It can be of no more use to you."

It was true. So I let Mochi dress me in a simple underrobe of unfinished silk and the kimono I had given her.

I felt I owed her something for her kindness. "You must promise to tell no one, Mochi-san," I said softly, "but I have been on a very strange journey indeed."

"Yes?" She leaned eagerly toward me.

"When my mother and sisters and brother and I fled the city, we were attacked on the road by robbers. My sister's husband, Yugiri, was killed."

"Ai. What a shame."

"I have been trying to learn what happened to Yugiri's soul since then."

"Why? Wasn't he properly buried?"

I paused, for that had not occurred to me. "I do not know. Some of our servants were to bring him home."

"Anyway," Mochi went on, "shouldn't it be your sister's place to pray for his soul?"

"It would be, but she cannot. She pines for him so, she will not move or speak."

"How strange. Why doesn't she just get another lover or husband?"

"How can you say such a thing?"

"You mean she loved her husband? Mama says the Good People trade lovers and spouses like we trade sacks of rice."

"I have heard those stories, too, but Amaiko is not like that."

"So. Go on. Where did you journey to?"

"I have been to holy places. I have seen Fuji-sama. And the island called Enoshima, where the Dragon King lives. I have been in the Court of Lord Emma-o and . . . other places."

"Amazing! And did you learn what happened to Yugiri's soul?"

"No. I was given a vision in the Temple of Kiyomizudera. I dreamed that Miroku, the Buddha Who Is Yet To Be, spoke to me. He told me that I must be brave, for the truth is horrible; yet I must search myself for the answer. I do not know what to make of this vision. I do not want to see any more horrible things. I wanted to come home, only my home is burned down. I feel so . . . lost."

"If you ask me, you should just wait for your father to come back, and forget about this Yugiri fellow. Let his more immediate family worry about him. You have your own life to look after."

"It is important. If you saw Amaiko, you would see how important it is."

"Life is important. The dead go where they go. They need no help from us."

"That is not so. If that were true, why would we chant sutras for the sick, or become monks when we're old?"

"*You* may chant sutras. *I* put a rice ball on the family shrine now and then and leave it at that."

I felt frustration then, for I had seen the other side of it. "They want you to remember them."

"Who?"

"Your ancestors. And they want to have news of this world."

"How would you know?"

I paused. "Another vision."

"Maybe you caught sick on the road, and that is why you had so many visions."

I sighed. "I knew you would not believe me."

Mochi shook her head. "You People from Above the Clouds live in such a different world. I never know what to believe from you. You live on poetry and perfume and glimpses of a person's sleeve. The real world doesn't exist for you."

"The real world is dirty and sinful and it is all illusion anyway. Why not live in elegance, apart from it?"

"Because the real world is more interesting."

Mochi's father returned then, with the rice farmers. They must have concluded some good business, for they were drunkenly singing together. Mochi's mother and brother bustled in and it became apparent that we were all going to sleep in the same room. I was very grateful for my kichō curtain, but still I was unnerved. How could these people live like this?

It took a while for the people to stop bustling around and for the pine-oil lamps to be blown out. I huddled, curled up on thin woven mats. The frayed straw made my skin itch wherever it touched me.

Tired as I was, I could not sleep. I was too aware of the strangeness of my surroundings. A loud snore was coming from Goranu's corner. A dog whimpered out in the street. The house smelled like cooked rice and sweat. How odd it was — to be in a home that felt so alien to me. I truly felt out of place. I did not belong here. And yet there was no place, at that moment, where I did belong. What a sad thing, I realized, to be no one and nowhere, like a —

I sat up, my heart pounding. I pushed the kichō aside and ran to where Goranu lay.

I shook his shoulder. "Goranu!" I whispered.

"Ummm?"

"Goranu! I know where Yugiri is!"

"That's good," the tengu murmured, and he tried to roll away.

"Goranu!" I shook him again. "We must go and help him."

"Tomorrow."

"We will not find him once the sun has risen. We must go now!"

"You go find him, then, and tell me all about it in the morning."

"No, it is far and you must take me there."

"Have you forgotten my feet?"

"Oh." I sat in a heap beside him. "Oh. I am so—I had—" I buried my face in my sleeves. I tried to cry softly, so as not to wake the others in the house.

"So, so, stop that now. I am only your tengu servant, after all, and naturally you forget my feelings."

"But Yugiri is in such a terrible place. And he has been there so long. The thought of him suffering so—"

"What about *my* suffering so? Anyway, which hell is it?"

"A hell that is here in this world."

Goranu paused. "This intrigues me, Little Puddle. I hope it is not some gibble-gabble you learned at the temple."

"No. I do not know why I did not think of it sooner."

"Sometimes things hide best in plain view. Does this new revelation answer the riddle of why Lord Emma-o claimed Yugiri was not dead?"

"Lord Emma-o did not say Yugiri lived. He said only that Yugiri had not come before him."

"Ah. I see. I had overlooked that." Goranu sat up. "So where will we find Yugiri?"

I told him.

"Ah. Yes. That would make sense." Goranu flopped onto his stomach. "Yes, I see." He turned onto his side. "It would answer everything." He rolled onto his back. "I wonder if you are right."

I sighed. "I suppose we cannot find out, since you cannot fly."

"Who said I can't fly? I can fly very well."

"But . . . your feet—"

"My feet? Oh, they will hurt a little. But I am a tengu. I heal quickly. See?" He unwrapped the bandages on his feet and illuminated them with a little blue flame in his hand. They were still big and ugly, but all the burned blackness was gone.

"But you told me you did not know if you would ever walk again."

"A creature in pain speaks all sorts of nonsense. Come, I am burning with curiosity and I must know. Let us go see Yugiri."

"You will fly me there?" I nearly cried out and clapped for joy, until I remembered the sleepers nearby. As he stood, I said, "Goranu, have you any bars of silver left?"

"Two."

"Please give them to me."

"Why?"

"Because I feel we owe our kind hosts something for leaving them so rudely."

"Oh. I was afraid you'd want to return them to the temple. Here you are."

I took the cool metal in my hands and stepped carefully to where Mochi lay. I slipped the bars into her hand.

"Mmmm?" She shifted a little in her sleep.

"Now you may tell your mama that you have at last traded the kimono for something more useful," I whispered. Then, as quietly as I could, I followed Goranu out into the street.

I could barely see him in the dim moonlight. His wings were black shadows on shadows. I leapt onto his back easily now and gripped his shoulder feathers.

"Ai! Ai! Ai! Ai! Ai! Ai!" he cried as he ran down the street. He jumped up, his wings beating the air.

Heian Kyō shrank swiftly beneath us as we rose, until it seemed a city for dolls. The night sky was immeasurably huge all around us, filled with glimmering stars. I felt more at home in the sky, on Goranu's back, than I had felt in Mochi's house. What a strange emotion that was.

By moonlight we followed the Western Road. From above, it was a pale silk ribbon draped carelessly over the hillsides. I watched the road carefully until the torchlight from the distant complex on Mount Hiei came into view.

"There!" I said, pointing down at the road.

Goranu spiraled down and I slid off his back just before his feet touched the earth. I got up from the dust and ran ahead to the curve in the road that had been burned into my memory. I was glad that we were not here in daylight, for the memories it might bring.

And there he was. I went up to him. "Yugiri."

He stared at me, amazed. "Mitsuko? You? I have been

waiting here, praying one of my kin would come for me. But I never thought it would be you."

I swallowed hard. "It is me. Only I know you are here."

"I saw your father and his servants pass this way some nights ago. I waved and yelled to them but they did not see me. How is it that you see me?"

"I have been looking for you."

"How is Amaiko?"

"She is like the Lady of the Orange Blossom House. She pines for you and will not eat or speak."

"Ah." Yugiri gazed up the road, rubbing his chest with his thumb. "So that is it. I can feel her pull upon me. I think she is part of the reason I remain here."

"Only part?"

His eyes turned to me sadly. "Yes, there is more. And I suppose I must show you, though it is not right that you should see it."

"I saw what befell us here, Yugiri. What could be worse?"

"True. Very well. Come this way, then."

I walked beside Yugiri back down the road toward the capital.

"Why is there a tengu following us?" said Yugiri.

"That is my friend, Goranu. He helped me find you."

"That is bad company, Little Sister. You should be more careful in choosing your playmates. He has not harmed you, has he?"

"Not at all. He is a good tengu."

"Can there be such a thing, I wonder?"

"I believe so."

We walked on in silence until Yugiri stopped. "Here I

am," he said. "Good tengu, if such you are, bring some light to this place."

"My name is Goranu, O Lofty Gentleman of Little Substance. And I will be happy to illuminate you."

A glowing ball of light appeared overhead, like a paper lantern hanging in midair. Yugiri became more indistinct, as if he were made of mist. Still I could see him pointing at the ground beside the road. There was a low dirt mound that had been disturbed on one side. An arm wearing torn black rags protruded from the earth. The hand had been gnawed on by animals.

"I cannot blame them, really," said Yugiri. "The servants who bore my body back toward home were afraid. For all they knew, the brigands might have come down the road to attack them again. It is harder to run when carrying a corpse. So they hastily buried me here, with no sutras chanted for my soul, no proper rites observed. At least I was the last to be dropped. The servants who died are scattered back up the road."

"How horrible," I said softly.

"There have been many long, empty days and nights since then, waiting here. But why you, Mitsuko?"

"For Amaiko's sake."

"Could she not come herself?"

"No." I did not wish to admit that I had left her in a tengu village. "But now that we have found you, Goranu and I will avenge you."

"You will?" said Yugiri.

"We will?" said Goranu.

"We will go to the gates of Hiei-zan and shame the priests into giving you proper burial."

"Mitsuko—"

"Little Puddle —"

"They owe you this!"

"Little Sister," said Yugiri, his face gravely patient in the moonlight, "would it not be better to tell your papa about all this and let him deal with the matter?"

"First," I said, "I do not know where Papa is. Second, you said he could not see you; so, third, why should he even believe me if I could find him and tell him?"

"A good argument," said Goranu.

"Very true, Little Sister," said Yugiri. "But you have no idea how arrogant the monks of Hiei-zan have become. You are a child. You are a *girl* child. Whyever would they listen to you?"

"Also a good argument," said Goranu.

I whirled to face him. "Have you become a cowardly fox now? You are a demon, neh? Where are your great powers?"

"Powers? You speak of tengu powers?" Goranu waved his arms. "We do jokes and japes and trick the eyes with illusions. We do not fence with swords, stab with knives, fling thunderbolts or fire, or even throw stones. Killing is for warriors and monks, not us."

"But have I not heard of some people dying from having believed tengu illusions?" said Yugiri.

"They die from their own folly," said Goranu. "But you would know of my powers, Little Puddle. Therefore I will use my tengu power to show you what you would be up against, were you to brave the gates of Hiei-zan. I will become the main gate and the gatekeepers. You tell me what you would tell the monks, and I will show you what their reaction would be."

To my amazement, Goranu whirled around, and where he had stood there grew a huge gateway in a high stone wall. I stared at it, speechless, for some moments.

"Well?" came Goranu's voice from behind the wall. "Say something. Who knocks at the gate of Hiei-zan?"

"I do." My voice was the squeak of a mouse.

"Who are you?"

"I am Fujiwara no Mitsuko, daughter of the Minister of the Inner Ward. I come seeking redress for a terrible thing done by your people."

"Indeed? A noble Lady, are you?" A young, shaven-headed monk appeared at the top of the wall beside the gate. "But you are all by yourself! Where are your servants? Where is your retinue? Have you no male relative to speak for you?"

My thoughts were knocked astray by his questions. "It is . . . I do not . . . That is not important. What matters is that your people have robbed my family, and my brother-in-law needs proper funeral rites, and you must perform them."

"What a strange request. You think we have robbed you, yet you come to us for services? You are either insane or a fool. Say, this wouldn't all be a trick so you could get inside to ply your business, would it? No women are allowed in Hiei-zan." Then he leaned forward and whispered loudly, "But pillow girls often can slip in through the north gate near the cooking pavilions. You might try there." Then he disappeared behind the wall, laughing.

I stood speechless.

Yugiri spoke behind me. "He is right, Mitsu-chan. That is very much the sort of welcome you would receive. The world is not so just and fair as we would have it."

"But it isn't right! Surely the monks at the real gate would know the truth of my claim."

"Given what they have done to our family, Mitsuko, I would not trust the warrior monks to have any sense of truth at all."

"Now you are talking sense," said Goranu. "A pity one must wait until death to gain such wisdom."

Yugiri smiled ruefully. "I had best watch my tongue if a tengu agrees with me. I would like my next destination to be better, not worse, than this one."

"Very well," I said. "I will not approach Hiei-zan's gate."

"Good for you," said Goranu.

"You, Goranu, will fly me into the very heart of the complex itself. That way they cannot possibly ignore me, and they will have to listen to what I say."

Goranu screeched and held his head. "Little Puddle, have you learned nothing? You saw what happened to my feet in Kiyomizudera. Think what will happen if I fly over a holy mountaintop. I will fall to the earth and be burned all over!"

I sighed and bowed my head. "Is there nothing I can do to set matters right?"

Yugiri said, "You could never redress the crime that has been done, Mitsuko, not even with your tengu friend. The world is very big and full of good and evil. Let those of greater power handle the greater matters. All I ask of you is that you rejoin your family, try to find someone to give me proper rites, and take care of Amaiko for me. Those are suitable tasks for you."

I stared at the ground. My fists were clenched and my

right foot was drawing lines in the dirt. "I do not know where the rest of our family is."

"Are they not at the mountain lodge?"

"The mountain lodge was ruined. Lord Tsubushima's men were coming for us when I and—when I ran away."

"Mitsuko, Mitsuko, how you complicate things! There has been a priest wandering by here now and then. Some nights, I think he almost sees me. He does not appear to be allied with any of the warrior temples nearby. Perhaps you could find him and ask if he has heard word of your family."

"Priest," muttered Goranu. "Pfui."

"Very well," I said; for, to be honest, I wished to leave Yugiri's company. After such a difficult search, to find him this way was so disappointing. He did not seem to want my help. I felt weak and useless. I went to Goranu and he obligingly dropped to one knee to let me on his back.

"Good-bye, Little Sister," said Yugiri. "Good luck to you. Be careful."

"Good-bye," I said softly.

Goranu ran up the road, his arms turning to great black wings. It was so expected now that I did not wonder at it. He jumped into the air and again the ground fell away from us. Tears blurred my sight of the Western Road.

"Why are you so sad, Little Puddle? You were right, and you have found your sister's husband's soul."

"To what use? Will it help Amaiko to know he is a ghost? In my vision in the temple, Miroku told me I would be able to set matters right. That is what I want to do."

"Ah, Little Puddle, sometimes I wish you were not quite

so brave. Wait. I smell a priest." He spiraled down again, sniffing the air.

At last we landed in sight of someone's campfire. We tried to be as quiet as possible as we approached the old man sitting by the fire. But he looked up before we were even close to him.

"It is Dentō!" I gladly ran up to him and knelt at his side.

"It is the lost Fujiwara girl," said Dentō, raising his brows. "Or one of them, at any rate. Where have you been? Where is your sister?"

"I have been searching for Yugiri's soul, Holy One. And I have found him!"

"Where— One moment." Dentō raised a sakaki branch and stared out past the fire. "Who are you and what do you want here?"

"Little Puddle, tell him who I am."

"That is Goranu. He is my friend and has been helping me."

"You have a tengu for a friend?"

"He came when I and Amaiko took shelter in a kami shrine. I asked the kami for forgiveness and to send help. Goranu was the help that arrived."

"How very curious. The divine powers do bewildering things indeed."

"Have you seen my mother, my sisters, and little Yūshō?"

"Alas, no, I cannot tell you how they are. I only know they are guests of Lord Tsubushima in his castle. He is a stern, shrewd commander, but he is not unnaturally cruel. I doubt that they have been harmed."

This did not much reassure me. "And my father? I have heard that he has passed this way."

"I saw some men on horseback, one a nobleman, riding at a gallop up the road the day before last. They passed so quickly, I did not get a good look at them."

"Ah."

"But please, tell me all that has happened with you. Clearly your story is more interesting than mine."

So again I told my story, even the fantastic things. Dentō listened with patience and did not dispute anything I said.

"Most amazing!" was all he replied when I had finished. "Miroku himself. Do you know how many of us wait for such a vision? Clearly you have the favor of the divine powers."

"Then why has my family had such bad fortune?"

"These events are on too large a scale for me to weigh them, Lady Mitsuko. There are forces tearing at the edges of our land that are unfathomable. Only the divine ones know the outcome. We must survive as we may. But you say you have found Yugiri's soul?"

I stared at the ground. "He is a ghost haunting this road. He was left without proper ritual not far from here. I spoke to him, offering to help, but he seemed not to want my help. So, although my search has ended, I am not content. I was told I could set matters right. Yet also I have been advised" — I glanced sidelong at Goranu across the fire — "that I am but a girl child and can do nothing."

"I am sure those who advised you were thinking only of your safety and well-being," said Dentō with a gentle smile. "But I understand your hunger for vengeance. I, too, have often felt the warrior monks deserved a lesson in humility.

Yet the temples of Hiei-zan have become enormously power-ful—more than any one person could face with effect. In this matter, we must be not the tiger who roars at the gate but the mouse who gnaws through the wall."

"Ah," said Goranu, "priestly wisdom, clear as the stormy sky."

"Please, Holy Sir," I said with a glare at Goranu, "what do you mean?"

"Well, it is clear what the kami must have had in mind in sending a tengu to you."

"Yes, Goranu has told me that it is a tengu's purpose and pleasure to harass monks. Yet he has refused to go to Mount Hiei."

"I understand. For that reason, Mount Hiei must come to us."

I blinked, quite confused.

"Monks can move mountains!" cawed Goranu. "They have become more powerful than I thought. What a boon for the country, when the Yin-Yang Ministers can have the world arranged like rocks in a garden."

Dentō coughed. "If I may beg patience of your demonic friend, Mitsuko-san, wait a moment and hear my thoughts. I think I can devise a strategy, with Goranu's help, that may interest you."

"Please, I will be happy to listen," I said.

And the three of us talked long into the night.

Little Sister of Illusion

When I sit just so,
the rain puddle beside me
can hold the moon.

$\mathcal{T}$HE EAST was beginning to fill with light when Goranu and I at last returned to his village. Sleepily I slid off his back as he alighted in the village street. The ground was damp with dew. A few morning birds sang on the hillsides. A faint light shone through one or two of the doorways. No one came out to greet us.

"Where is everyone?"

"Most of my kin will have just gone to bed," said Goranu.

"Then I suppose we should, too," I said with a yawn. I pulled my kimonos tight around me against the chill air.

One of the door curtains was flung aside and someone

peered out. The person made a high-pitched cry and came running toward us.

"It appears one of your womenfolk has at last noticed our presence," I said.

Goranu frowned. "She is not of my kind."

The woman kept running stiffly, arms outstretched. She did not stop running or keening until she had careened into me, knocking me backward into Goranu. She grasped me in a tight embrace, her face buried in my shoulder. At last I heard words in her cries— "Mitsu-chan, Mitsu-chan," she said, over and over.

The scent of her hair was familiar, though too strong. "Amaiko?"

She responded with sobs. Tears formed in my eyes also. She stepped back, still clutching my shoulders. In the dim morning light, it hardly seemed to be her. Her face was terribly thin and there were dark circles below her eyes. Her hair was bedraggled and she clearly had not bathed in a while.

"What have they done to you?" I whispered.

"Dear Little Sister, come inside. It is so cold. Come inside and I will tell you."

I let her guide me to the hut she had emerged from. The central hearth gave a little warmth. One lamp hung from a rafter gave light—Amaiko looked even worse. Goranu followed, now in young man shape, behind us.

"You aren't becoming a tengu, are you?" I said.

Amaiko laughed. "I hope not. It has been hard enough becoming human again."

I sat beside her and we held each other. "I found Yugiri."

"What?"

"That must be why your soul has returned, neh? Because I found him."

"Yugiri is dead, Mitsu-chan."

"Yes, I know."

She tilted her head and regarded me. "Poor thing. Talking nonsense. It has been a difficult time for us." She gently moved a lock of my hair off of my forehead.

I did not know what to tell her. *She might not believe me. It might not be kind of me to tell her.* So I said nothing.

"Let me tell you what has happened to me," said Amaiko, her arm around my shoulders. "I remember dreams of a ruined house, of running through a forest, of trying to sleep in a small, cold place. Then there was wind, and the sound of many birds. I remember floating like an autumn leaf."

"You never saw Yugiri?"

"I thought I did once, in the darkness. He seemed so sad. But that was many dreams ago. When I at last awoke, I was in this place. I was very hungry. Ravenous. The first thing I saw clearly was a bowl of rice. It was within grasp and I reached for it. Then an ugly woman scuttled up to me and pulled the bowl away, placing it just out of my reach. 'You want this?' she said to me. 'You will have to crawl for it.' I reached out for it again, and she pulled it away again. As she said she would, she made me crawl across the floor after the bowl before she finally let me eat."

I glared at Goranu. "You said she would be well cared for! Beasts! I should never have left Amaiko here."

"Perhaps you should let her finish," said Goranu.

"Before long," Amaiko went on, "I had to do the

necessary thing. But I hated the ugly creatures cackling around me and I dared not embarrass myself before them. So I managed to crawl outside the hut. They taunted me, saying what a baby I was. I was so angry, I had to prove them wrong. So I stood and walked. They taunted my clothing, so I made sure my gowns hung properly. They taunted my silence until I screamed the most horrible words at them. They said you had deserted me, so I waited with patient pride."

I looked aghast at Goranu. He simply nodded, as if it were no less than what he had expected. I lunged at him. "You monster! You awful, horrible creature! You knew they would do this to her!" I beat at him with my fists.

"Wait! Wait, Little Puddle!" he cried, hiding behind his big black sleeves. "You don't understand yet!"

"Understand? I understand I have been tricked! You took me away so that your awful women could torment my sister!"

Amaiko grabbed my arms and pulled me off Goranu. "He is right, Mitsuko. There is more to tell. That was only the first day after my awakening. The two days after that, they taunted me less and encouraged me more. These women helped me come back to the world and regain my pride. I . . . I am grateful to them."

"You see, Little Puddle," said Goranu, "so long as your sister was cared for by you, she did not need to awaken to the world. The only way to get her spirit back was to take you from her, so that she would have to return to save herself."

I felt very cold. I looked at Amaiko.

"He is right, Mitsu-chan. You were a very sweet nursemaid. But you would have let me wallow in my grief forever.

I know the old poems say that is proper for a widow, but it would not be fair to you. I loved Yugiri and I will always miss him. But there must be a reason I was left in this world when he was not."

Hurt seemed to blossom inside me, though I could not say why. I had had to abandon my sister in order for her to heal. Had my kindness before harmed her? Was I so useless as that?

Goranu shook my shoulder. "Do not fall into the well of self-pity, Little Puddle. You were important. You brought your sister to us. You kept her from the castle of Lord Tsubushima, where she would have languished until death. Now, remember, we have other important things to do. You are tired. Get some sleep so we will be ready for tonight."

"Tonight?" said Amaiko.

Goranu grinned beneath his big nose. "We are going to take revenge on some monks tonight."

Amaiko gasped. "What will you do? Is there any way I may help?"

My feelings then were most bizarre. I was angry, as if something was being stolen from me. "No, Amaiko. You are too weak. You must stay here until you are better."

"Too weak? For what, Mitsuko? You aren't going to fight them, are you?"

"No, no, no," said Goranu, his eyes wide. "Nothing like that, my Lady. We will simply do an illusion."

"An illusion? Such as those performed at the temple dances? I have been told I am talented at dancing. Can this help you?"

"No," I said.

Goranu looked at me strangely. "Well, in fact, my Lady, one more person, particularly a female one, might indeed be of use, although dancing will not be required."

"Then I must come with you," said Amaiko.

"I do not see why," I said.

Amaiko regarded me sadly. "For Yugiri. He was my husband."

I realized I was behaving terribly. How could I deny her? "Yes. Very well. Of course you must come."

"So," said Goranu, "we are decided. Now get some sleep."

I curled up on the floor, feeling a sick sourness inside.

Amaiko brushed my hair and I wept myself to sleep. It was strange to be sleeping during the day, like an old woman.

> *The bloom returns*
> *to my favorite cherry tree.*
> *Why, then, am I sad?*

> *Because I was not tending*
> *the garden where she blossomed?*

> *Because her leaves may*
> *keep the sun from shining on*
> *the new growth below?*

When I at last rose again, it was late afternoon. I ached all over and felt very out of sorts. I ate little and spoke little to anyone, while Goranu and Amaiko gathered what was needed. As the sun crept below the mountains to the west, we prepared to leave the village. I felt an odd pride because I easily climbed onto Goranu's back as he took bird form. Amaiko protested that she could never do such a terrifying thing, and so two tengu had to carry her in a net slung between them.

As we flew back to the Western Road, Amaiko had to bite on her fingers to keep from shrieking in fear. *I was right*, I thought. *She should not have come with us.* This pleased me in a way that I think was not kind.

We cast long shadows on the dirt of the road as we landed. I had to hold Amaiko for some moments to still her trembling. "You are so very brave," she said to me. "How could you do this many times and not go mad?"

"I . . . I have come to rather enjoy it, Amaiko."

She stared as if madness was already upon me.

"Come, come," said Goranu, herding us with his wings. "Dentō awaits in the woods, and he will curse us or something if we make him wait too long."

We hurried into the clearing where we had talked with the old priest the night before. He stood to hush us, then stopped and stared at Amaiko. "My Lady, you have returned!"

She decorously hid her face. "Holy Sir, I do not think we have met. Why do you address me so?"

I tugged on her sleeve. "He saw you while your mind was . . . elsewhere," I whispered.

"You let him look at me in such a state?"

"He was trying to heal you, Amaiko."

"Is that why I found ashes and bits of leaves in my hair, and why my kimonos stink of incense?"

"We hoped he could bring you back."

"Really, Mitsuko, how could you or Mama allow such a thing?"

I sighed. Goranu clacked his beak and growled, "Can't we talk about this later? We must prepare."

"They will be coming down this side path within the hour," said Dentō. "They are most likely not the same monks who attacked your wagons, but they will be affiliated with those. I have met these fellows often. Therefore get you in place quickly, before they arrive."

I shall describe what unfolded that evening in the way that the Hiei monks themselves must have seen it, for I think that will be more interesting.

Five monks came down a path from Mount Hiei. They often did so at sunset, to see what they could catch by hunting. Or perhaps they might find an unfortunate traveler to rob. But on this particular evening, they encountered the old priest, Dentō, running up the path to greet them.

"Brothers!" the old priest cried. "I have just seen the most amazing thing!"

The monks looked at each other in wonder. Although Dentō was not of their sect, he was known to be wise and venerable. "What is it, Holy One? Tell us."

"You must come with me and tell me if my old eyes can be trusted, but there are two beautiful kami in the road, and they speak to me of treasure."

The monks, having no other plans for entertainment, readily agreed to accompany the old priest. They continued down the path until it met the Western Road. There they, indeed, saw two beautiful female bodhisattvas — one tall, one short; surrounded by a glowing, pearly radiance; wearing shimmering gowns that rippled where there was no wind.

"Greetings, Well-Favored Ones," said the visions, in haunting, elegant voices. "Be joyous, for we come to tell you of a precious treasure."

The monks looked at one another. "Can we believe such a sight?"

"It might be a tengu trick."

"Brothers," said Dentō, "you know I am old and have seen many things. I have learned how to discern a tengu illusion. And I tell you that these creatures are unquestionably real."

"Believe him," I — that is, the shorter bodhisattva — said. "You have proven yourselves daring and worthy. Nearby is a hidden treasure that we know you will put to proper use. Follow us."

"What can we lose?" said the monks to each other. "Let us see where they lead."

And so the five monks and Dentō followed the shining bodhisattvas down the Western Road. Presently they came to a dirt mound at the side of the road. Gold and silver gleams escaped through cracks in the mound, suggesting that great wealth lay within.

"Here," said the taller bodhisattva. "Dig into this earth and receive that which you deserve."

The monks could scarcely restrain themselves. Yet one said, "Dentō — you must take the first handful of treasure, for you were so generous as to share this vision with us."

"No!" said the smaller bodhisattva. "This treasure is not for him, because he . . . is tainted in his beliefs. Only you, dwellers of Hiei-zan, are worthy."

"It is true," Dentō said, nodding. "I have allowed odd ways to creep into my practices, as you, my brothers, know. And I have taken a vow against acquiring wealth. Please feel free to partake of this yourselves. It may bring your temple much good."

"Yes, yes, the temple," the monks said to each other. "We must think of the temple. It would be wrong of us to ignore this holy gift." So they eagerly jumped upon the earthen mound and began to dig with their hands. With cries of joy, they lifted out slender bars of silver and gold held together with silken cords, and raised them up to view.

As suddenly as a candle blows out, that part of the illusion vanished. The monks now held bones connected with bits of flesh and cloth. With loud shrieks, they dropped the moldering things and rubbed their hands on their robes.

But it was too late. For, you see, every monk toils many years learning and writing sutras for the enlightenment and furtherance of his soul. But to touch something so unclean as a corpse wipes out all the years of worthy effort, and makes it all for nothing. Each monk now would have to do years of holy work just to ensure that his next life would not be worse than his current one.

"Why have you done this to us?" they exclaimed. "This is no treasure!"

"A great crime was committed here, by members of your temple," said the smaller bodhisattva. "We have indeed brought you to a treasure, for these remains are precious to the families of the dead. And you now have the opportunity to make amends for a great wrong."

"What must we do?"

"See that these are given the proper rites."

The monks bobbed up and down like feeding cranes. "Yes, yes, we will bury their ashes in the holy ground of Mount Hiei."

"No," said the taller bodhisattva. "You must take them to their family cemetery in Heian Kyō."

"What family is that?"

"None other than the Fujiwara."

"The Fujiwara!" The monks backed away. "They would have us arrested and killed!"

"Then you had better treat their remains with reverence," said the taller one, "so as to better prepare for your next life."

"And if you do not do as we say," said the shorter one, "you will all become frogs in your next existence." Dentō frowned at this, but I thought it was very clever.

So, slowly, the monks gathered up the bones, putting them in the sacks they had hoped to fill with loot. "Take special care with those," said the taller bodhisattva. "He was . . . a very good man."

"Yes, yes," said the monks, and they slung the full sacks over their backs and trotted down the Western Road toward the capital. I saw Yugiri following behind them. He nodded to me once, then gazed with longing for a moment at Amaiko. She looked in his direction but did not seem to see him. Yugiri turned away, eyes downcast, and followed the monks who bore his bones.

"Amaiko," I said.

She was staring at the ground and shivering.

"Did you see him?"

"See whom?"

"Never mind. It is nothing."

Goranu and two other tengu came out from the trees behind us, laughing and whooping with glee. "Did you see those monks' faces! Oh, how unhappy they were when they found the gold was only bones. They will be lucky to come back as worms next time, neh?"

Goranu said to us, "Excellent work, my Ladies! You would make fine tengu indeed."

Amaiko did not deign to reply to that. I was pleased, however, that the trick went so well and that some small amount of justice had been served.

"As for you, Dentō," Goranu went on, "never did I think I would enjoy working with a monk, but you are an unusual fellow. Come back to our village and celebrate with us."

"You honor me too much," said Dentō, "but I fear I must decline. While Yugiri is at last being looked after, there are those servants whose remains were left by the road. They are also in need of proper rites. I must do what I can for them. Good-bye, Goranu-san. Fare you well, Ladies."

We bowed and thanked him for his help, although I confess I was confused as to why he should concern himself with the souls of mere servants.

When we returned to the tengu village, Goranu and his two fellow demons stayed up much of the night, recounting their skillful illusion to the others. Amaiko and I held each other a long while before we finally went to sleep.

Little Sister of Spirit

An egg holds a bird,
a chrysalis holds a moth.
What do I contain?

$\mathcal{T}$HE SUN was too bright when I awoke. I sought the shadows of the hut in which to eat my morning rice. Amaiko was quiet also, but I think she was worrying about Yugiri. There was a noise at the doorway to the hut and I nearly dropped my bowl. Goranu pounded in, wearing young man shape, flinging the door curtain aside.

"Good morning, Ladies! Are you ready to go home at last?"

"Good morning," Amaiko murmured decorously. She raised a sleeve before her face. I thought it was a rather silly gesture—he was only Goranu, after all.

"Go home?" I said. "We do not have a home. It burned down. Don't you remember?"

Amaiko put down her rice suddenly and stared at me. "Burned down?"

"Oh." I looked away. "I forgot to tell you."

"Our house in Heian Kyō?"

"Yes."

"Papa-chan?"

"He was not there when it burned, I was told."

Amaiko gazed at the floor. "How many miseries follow us! Where is Papa, then?"

"I do not know."

Goranu put on a smug smile. "Ah, but I do."

"Do you?" said Amaiko. "Where?"

It was the strangest thing, but I did not want to know. I did not want Goranu to speak. I did not want to think about such things as family and the future.

"Some of my cousins saw him and his servants outside of Lord Tsubushima's castle. Your mother, sisters, and brother are inside, but Lord Tsubushima will not let your father see them."

"Why not?"

"He is trying to weasel your father into giving up some land in exchange for them, I hear."

"Oh, how terrible," said Amaiko. "Why haven't the rest of our clan sent help?"

"I expect," said Goranu, "the various groups of monks in the capital are keeping the Imperial forces busy. A pity, because the bulk of Lord Tsubushima's army is also elsewhere, putting down rebellion in his province. Still, there are enough bowmen guarding the castle that we cannot take you there. But we can set you near your father."

I felt angry then, and came forward into the light. "Yes, we should go to Papa."

"Yes," said Amaiko. "I suppose we must. Though there is little we can do for him. Perhaps just seeing us and knowing we are well will give him heart."

"We can do more than that," I said.

Amaiko paused and said, "Do you think poetry might sway Lord Tsubushima's heart?"

"I was not thinking that at all."

"Lord Tsubushima," said Goranu, "is not a very cultured man."

"Then whatever could *we* do? — Oh, Mitsu-chan, you are not suggesting that we offer ourselves in marriage in exchange, are you? That is terribly brave and self-sacrificing, though I do not think — "

"No, no, no!" I wanted to beat my fists on the hard wooden floor. "That is not necessary! Do you not see? Papa needs an army. We will bring him an army."

Amaiko blinked. "Whatever are you talking about?"

I looked at Goranu. "It does not have to be a real army, if Lord Tsubushima's men are away. It just has to look like one."

Goranu's eyes widened. "Are you suggesting that we do another illusion for you?"

"Yes! It would be simple, neh?"

"Mitsuko!" Amaiko motioned for me to come near her. Reluctantly, I did. She whispered in my ear, "We should have little more to do with these demons. Yes, they have helped us, but we are doing ourselves spiritual harm. They are not trustworthy friends. Let us speak no more of illusions, neh?"

I pulled away from her. "What do you think, Goranu? Is it possible?"

"Hmmm. You don't understand, Little Puddle. My kind will gladly do anything to upset monks. But what you suggest has nothing to do with monks. I don't think I could talk my cousins into it."

Amaiko gave me a "There, you see?" look.

"But all of this began with the monks."

Goranu gazed at me sadly. "All of this began when mankind learned greed and ambition."

"You are beginning to speak like a Buddhist," said Amaiko.

"I am?" said Goranu, shocked. "Ai! ai! Now look what you have made me do! Now I shall have an aching head all day!"

"Then do the illusion. It will make you wicked again and take away your headache. And tell your tengu cousins that such a large illusion would be truly a test of their skill. Tell them . . . tell them my sister and I doubted their magic. Tell them we think the monks, or the Dragon King, can do better."

"Ow! ow! I will speak to them," said Goranu. Holding his head, he ran out through the door curtain.

Amaiko tilted her head and regarded me. "You have changed."

"Hmmmm?"

"I do not think I like this change. You have become most . . . unladylike."

"Whatever do you mean?" I asked.

"Well, for example, you did not cover your face when he entered."

"He is only a tengu!"

"Even so."

"And he has seen *your* face plenty of times already."

"That does not matter. I was unaware of it and unable to stop it. You see? That is a difference. A lady must uphold the proprieties whenever she is able. And to be talking of armies and magic . . . I do not think Papa will be pleased, Mitsuko."

"But I want to help him!"

"Your help will be better appreciated if it is more subtle. If you are ever to serve at Court, you must understand this."

I looked out past the door curtain. "I think I do not wish to serve at Court."

"Mitsuko! How can you say such a thing? How else do you think you can bring honor to our family? Remember, you are a Fujiwara."

I fidgeted with the edge of my sleeve. I did not look at her. I did not want to hear what she was saying.

"It is all well and good," Amaiko went on, "for a child to say brash and bold things — it will be forgiven. But you are growing up, Mitsuko. Before long, you will marry someone important and, if you are fortunate, have children of your own. You must pay better attention to your behavior."

So many thoughts were in my mind. I'd thought Amaiko was my friend, and she was treating me like a child. And I feared she was right, in a way. If I returned to my family, that was what would be expected. What else could I do? But after flying in the clouds above Fuji-sama, how could I return to the shut-in world of a noble lady? I could not imagine it. Naturally, Amaiko did not understand. During my adventures, she was elsewhere — they had not touched her.

I tried to change the direction of conversation. "Do you want to know what happened when Goranu returned me to the capital? We found the house had burned, and none of our neighbors would take me in."

"Oh, how sad."

"So I stayed with Mochi and her family."

"Who is . . . Mochi? Is that some silly nickname?"

"She is the rice cake girl who sometimes takes food to the Palace."

"You stayed . . . in the home of a rice cake maker?"

"They were very kind."

"Mitsuko! You should not have done this!"

"She was the only one who offered lodging to me."

"Well, that is unfortunate. It was foolish of you to accept. You could have found someone else. You must never tell our family about this."

"But I must tell them. I promised Mochi. We should help her family in return."

"But they only — Mitsu-chan, you are — you are yet young and unsophisticated. You know nothing about people. You are fortunate they did not decide to hold you for ransom, or some other horrible thing."

"They were very kind."

"It is my fault. I should have taught you more than just the koto and poetry and how to wear your clothes. There is more to being a lady of quality than these, and the best women come by their grace naturally. But let us talk no more of this. Really, Mitsuko, I think you are deliberately trying to shock me. You must think of something else to tell Papa." Amaiko became very interested in picking rice grains off her kimono.

We did not speak to each other for at least an hour after that.

In the afternoon, Goranu returned in old man form. "Ho, Ladies, I have good news!"

"Who are you?" asked Amaiko.

"It is just Goranu again," I said with a sigh.

"This is most annoying," said Amaiko. "You tengu change shape so often, I cannot tell if I have already met you or not. Please stand outside. I will not be familiar with one who is always a stranger."

Goranu made a face at me and stepped outside the door curtain.

I was furious with Amaiko. "He is our friend!"

"He is *your* friend, and an odd choice of friends, at that."

"There is something I do not understand," said Goranu from outside. "If you Ladies of the Court never see your suitors, how do you know who is courting you? Or if it is not different men wearing the same scent or speaking in the same voice."

Amaiko raised her chin. "We know."

"Do you? Do you know who is speaking with you at any time, my plum blossom, my ginkgo leaf?" With a shock, I realized Goranu's voice had become very like Yugiri's.

Amaiko's face went pale. "You are cruel."

"Yes. I am a tengu and we are sometimes cruel. We just can't help it."

Amaiko stared at me. "And this is your friend."

To my own surprise, I stood and walked out through the door curtain. Amaiko called my name, but I ignored her. Goranu raised his brows as I walked up to him.

"That was unfair of you," I said.

Old man Goranu looked a little sheepish. "She was being pompous. We tengu hate pomposity."

"She is my sister."

"She called me a Buddhist this morning!"

"It was for her that I have made this long journey. I request that you please apologize to her."

Goranu let out his breath in a long sigh. "Then, for your sake, brave Little Puddle, I will do so. A thousand pardons, I beg, Lady Amaiko, for my unkind trick."

Within the hut, Amaiko said:

> *One need not forgive*
> *the fly that flits and buzzes*
> *over one's rice bowl.*

Goranu winced. "Now who is being unkind?"

"If you please," I said, "you said you had good news for us."

"Indeed. I was able to convince my brethren to undertake one more illusion on your behalf. They are proud of their skill and are itching to show it off. We will fly you to your father this afternoon."

"Fly!" came Amaiko's voice. "Must I be bound like a butterfly in a net again? Have you no more civilized way to travel?"

"I suppose you could walk, my Lady, but it is many ri to where your father waits. You do not seem the sort to be used to long walks."

"Have you no carriages?"

"We are tengu. We have no need of carriages, and besides, we tend to frighten horses and oxen. It's walk or fly, that's all."

"Then I suppose I must fly," she said.

"Good," said Goranu.

"It is only once more," I added, to soothe her. And then my very words struck me. Only once more to go riding on a bird's back and feel like a kami of the wind. Only once more to see the world stretch out below me, an endless brocade of mountains and rivers. I turned to Goranu, not knowing what I would say . . . but he was already trotting back to his fellows.

We departed as the sun was touching the peak of Mount Kurama. I paid no attention to Amaiko's fearful sighs, but tried to take in with my eyes the glory of the view below us. The capital glittered like a jewel dropped into a garment of vermillion silk. And the sky . . . Ah, the sky! How I wished I could sport among those gold and purple clouds as dragons do. I prayed that the Amida would not let me forget such a wondrous sight.

The tengu set us down in the road near Lord Tsubushima's castle, but not in sight of it. "Your father and his servants are in the grove around that bend," Goranu said. "We will be waiting for your signal."

I slid off his back and helped Amaiko out of the net. Together we ran down the road — and there was Papa, pacing up and down beneath a grove of plum trees. One of the servants stood up and exclaimed as he saw us. Papa turned, stared in shock, and then opened his arms.

"My children, my children!" he gasped as we embraced him. "Did Lord Tsubushima set you free? Did you escape?"

"We were never with him," said Amaiko.

I opened my mouth to speak; but words were difficult, my tears choked me so. "We . . . ran away . . . before they came for us. Oh, Papa-chan." I sobbed into his sleeve. Being with him made me feel almost as though the horrors of the weeks past had never happened.

Then he stepped back to look at us. And I saw how he had changed. He was thinner, and the creases were deeper in his face. His hair held more gray, and his eyes had never seemed so sad. "Oh, Ama-chan, Mitsu-chan, can you ever forgive me? I should never have let you travel so unprotected. I only thought . . . I only thought they would leave the innocent alone. Such a fool I was. Such a fool."

"How could you have known?" said Amaiko.

"But what has happened with you?" said Papa. "Where have you been all this time?"

"Did you not get Mama's letters?" I asked.

Papa's face went hard. "I heard nothing until a messenger found me some days ago to tell me that Tsubushima had taken my family in for protection and was suggesting I might want to give some of the Fujiwara estate to him in exchange for their safekeeping."

"We were attacked on the road," said Amaiko, "and Yugiri . . . was killed." She gazed at the ground.

"So I eventually learned," said Papa softly. "It is impossible to express my sorrow for your loss, Amaiko. He was like an elder son to me."

"We went to the mountain lodge," I said, "as you instructed us, but it was in terrible repair."

"I have seen it," Papa said. "Tsubushima has much to answer for."

"Tsubushima-sama kept trying to get us to stay at his castle. Finally we ran out of food and things to trade. We had heard nothing from you, so Mama felt we had no choice."

Papa nodded. "And you escaped from his men?"

"I ran away before they came for us. I took Amaiko with me. She was . . . She—"

"I was in no condition to protest," said Amaiko.

"I understand," Papa said.

"So we ran away," I went on, "and eventually we were guided to a village in the forest."

My father nodded again. "I should have come up to the mountains sooner, but I let politics delay me. In the end, it did not matter. Our house . . . our house was burned by vandals shortly after I left."

"Yes. We know."

"Do you?"

Amaiko cast a warning glance at me.

"We . . . heard from one of the villagers who had been to the capital."

"Ah. He had tried to bring a letter to me, no doubt."

I did not deny my father's misunderstanding, but I did not add to it. The lie made me uncomfortable and I wondered why I should say such a thing.

"But you must tell me which village has shown you such

kindness. There are few villages of any size in this part of the province. Tell me which one, and I will see they are rewarded, however I may."

"Um, it is hidden and its people are secretive. We have been asked not to reveal its location."

Papa narrowed his eyes. "Are they monks?"

"Oh, no! They are enemies of Hiei-zan."

"Hm. Good. Still, I owe them gratitude for looking after you. Somehow I must send a letter and gift to the headman of the village."

"It may be that you will have a chance to meet him."

"Indeed? Under what circumstances?"

"We . . . have heard from the villagers that the main part of Lord Tsubushima's army is elsewhere."

"Your friends are able spies. But the distance of his forces is of little good to us. I have no army but our trusted servants. They can hardly be expected to battle his castle guard. I have sent word to the Minister of War requesting men, but I doubt that my message will reach him. And even if it should, they have enough to contend with in the capital. I fear negotiation is my only course of action."

"Papa-chan," I said, "the villagers have heard of your terrible position. They wish to be our allies, for they have no love for Lord Tsubushima. They are willing to offer their warriors in our aid."

Papa stared at me. "Is this true? This is amazing news, if so. But do they have men enough, and are they trained? I fear an outlying village may not be as powerful as it believes."

"If you wish, you may judge for yourself. Shall I summon them?"

Papa tilted his head and regarded me as though I were a strange, unknown flower he had found in his garden. "Summon them? Can you do such a thing, Mitsuko?"

I felt it best not to answer, so I merely smiled. I pulled out of my sleeve a wooden whistle that Goranu had given me and I blew two notes upon it. Then I turned and watched down the road.

We heard them before we saw them—the soft clopping of many horses' hooves on the dirt road, the jingling of their harnesses, the creaking of saddles and armor. Then the army came around the bend.

The tengu "warriors" rode on steeds blacker than night, whose eyes held a red, demonic glow. The warriors, dressed in armor of black lacquer and red cords, wore battle masks carved in the guise of hawks' beaks. Their long banners were yellow, bearing the emblem of a raven. Behind the first ranks, they carried torches. More and more emerged around the bend—there seemed no end of them. They rode slowly, silently, proudly to where Papa-chan stood. The first one held up a dark glove and they halted.

Amaiko whispered in my ear, "I thought he said they made horses nervous."

"Hush," I said. "I want to hear them."

"Greetings, Fujiwara-sama," said the lead warrior. "Long have your clan been esteemed with the greatest respect and reverence by my people. Your brave daughters tell us you have need, and so we come."

Papa stared openmouthed, such that I found it hard to keep from laughing. "I offer greetings in return. It is a great joy to find such good friends in this wilderness. When my daughter spoke of you, I feared you might be a small, rough band. But now my misapprehensions have vanished. May I know your name and your people?"

The lead warrior said in a low, commanding voice, "I am Lord Goranu."

I had to stifle myself with my sleeves.

"My people choose to live in peaceful secrecy, therefore I cannot reveal our name. But your plight has moved us, and we will do our utmost to aid you in the return of your family."

"This is most mysterious," said Papa. "Yet I am grateful for your assistance. I am surprised Lord Tsubushima is not aware of you."

"He does not know of our existence."

"And the warriors of Hiei-zan?"

"They have some knowledge of us. We harass them from time to time."

"Then, indeed, you are welcome allies. Wait and I will join you. Together we will see if Tsubushima will change his demands."

"We await you." Lord Goranu bowed.

Papa had his servants bring his gray stallion and he mounted up beside the tengu. Proudly, he positioned his horse beside "Lord" Goranu. He looked wonderfully brave. I did not know whether to laugh or to sigh with admiration.

With a call to the riders behind him that sounded like the cry of a raven, Goranu moved forward. The warriors replied with an echoing cry that made my hair stand on end, and then they followed.

I turned and Amaiko grabbed my shoulders. "No, Mitsuko, don't!" she said. But I pulled away from her and ran alongside the road, back where Papa could not see me. I had to find out what would happen.

They stopped some yards before the mighty wooden gates and stone walls of the castle. The men at the top of the wall stared down at them. I peeked through the trees—the tengu warriors filled the road as far back as I could see, their torches glimmering. I could not tell how much was real and how much illusion. And, I hoped, neither could Lord Tsubushima's men.

"Who are you? What do you want?" called down a sentry from the castle wall.

"Summon Lord Tsubushima, and tell him Fujiwara no Munetame brings him answer to his offer."

One of the men on the wall ran off. As I waited, I gazed up at the sky. Low, heavy clouds rolled toward the castle. Thunder boomed among them, and when lightning flickered in their depths, I thought I saw the forms of dragons. *Did Goranu get the Dragon King to help as well? How wonderful!*

A tall bearded man appeared on the castle wall. He stared out over the army before his gates. Even from a distance, I could tell by the way he paced back and forth along the wall that he was confused and worried. "Munetame-san," he called down, at last.

"Tsubushima-san," said Papa, bowing in his saddle slightly less than would be polite.

"You should have sent word ahead of your arrival," said Lord Tsubushima. "I regret that I cannot possibly be hospitable to so many. My castle is too small and my resources too few. I may not open my gates to you."

"I understand, Tsubushima-san. Please forgive my lack of notice, but my . . . allies arrived but a short time ago."

"Who are these allies you have brought? I do not recognize their insignia, the raven."

Papa smiled and said, "The Fujiwara have made many friends over the centuries that we have given service to the Imperial family. Not all of them live in Heian Kyō. But I understand your ignorance. Here in a faraway, mountainous province, you could not possibly keep track of all that is important."

I knew Papa was speaking insults sent like finely barbed arrows to stick into Lord Tsubushima's pride, and I laughed behind my sleeves.

He went on. "This is Lord Goranu, and his people are of an ancient and fierce warrior clan. They live in the mountains and gain their skill from battling the monks of Hiei-zan. They know the Fujiwara are the enemies of Hiei-zan, and Lord Goranu's people have vowed to assist us against any who would aid, or take advantage of, the treachery of the warrior monks."

A low growl rose among the tengu warriors, echoing off the castle walls until the world seemed full of angry sound. This was followed by a loud clatter, as of sword sheaths against armor, or the rattle of large beaks. Some of the tengu lifted their banners high, the cloth rippling and snapping in the wind, fluttering like new-kindled flames.

"No one could blame you, Tsubushima-san," said Papa, "for being unable to offer hospitality to so great an army as this. Fortunately, we do not seek food or lodging from you. But I am given to understand that you have offered lodging to my wife, my son, and my daughters, for their safekeeping. You have my gratitude. But, as you can see, I am now able to provide for their safety myself. Therefore, please send out my family to me, and we will trouble you no further."

Lord Tsubushima began to pace the wall again. This was a dangerous moment, full of portent. A long, heavy silence fell over us all.

Should the provincial lord have chosen to be stubborn, I do not know what Goranu and Papa would have done.

And then a storm wind arose, whipping my hair, fluttering the war banners, and blowing the dragon clouds ever closer. Thunder rolled among them and Lord Tsubushima looked up at the darkening sky.

Dragons lowered their great heads out of the billowing black clouds, and lightning played between their enormous claws.

"What is this?" cried Lord Tsubushima, above the thunder.

Goranu replied, "More allies come at the call of the Fujiwara! Many times has that illustrious family done a service for the Dragon King of the Sea. Now minions of the Dragon King have come to serve the Fujiwara!"

I could see Papa-chan was trying very hard not to look surprised, but he did glance over his shoulder at the sky.

The other fighters on the castle wall were clearly afraid, and they shouted at Lord Tsubushima, pointing at the clouds.

"Good Munetame-sama," Lord Tsubushima called down, "you have given me more than enough reassurance that you can protect your family. It would be dishonorable of me to be an impediment to your reunion any longer. As you will see, your wife and children have been treated with all due respect and care. If you will but wait a moment, I will have them brought out to you."

"I thank you, Tsubushima-san. I will forget those rumors I have heard that you were keeping my kin hostage for reasons of personal gain. Surely they were incorrect. Such acts could only be imagined of a less cultured man than you. I eagerly await my family's return, as, you understand, I have not seen them in some while."

"Then wait no longer, Munetame-sama. I shall send them out at once." Lord Tsubushima bowed deeply and disappeared from the castle wall. In but a few minutes, the great wooden gates of the castle opened a crack. Two women and a little boy hurried through and then the gate was quickly shut again.

They ran up to Papa on his horse, and grasped his leg, calling out to him. I had to get closer to him to be sure . . . Yes, it was Mama, and Kiwako and little Yūshō. They were all talking at once. "It is you!" "You've truly come!" "Why did you take so long?" "Didn't you get my letters?" "Who are these men?" "Where did the dragons come from?" "Why did you send us to that ruined house?" "Papa! Papa!" "Did you hear about Yugiri?" "Have you seen Mitsuko and Amaiko?" "Why didn't you come sooner?" "We missed you so!"

Papa was reaching down, touching them, holding their hands, saying their names and, "I am so sorry. Are you well? Has he harmed you? No? My precious ones. How good to see you. I should never have left you."

I could not help myself then. I rushed out of the bushes to greet Mama, and Amaiko (who must have followed me) came running up also. We all embraced one another and again asked many questions—mostly to hear each other's voices, for none of the questions were answered.

"Where have you been?" "Are you well?" "Look at you, you're a mess!" "Amaiko—you're awake!" "No one hurt you?" "Mitsuko! Where are your clothes?" "So good to see you." "So good to see you." "So good to see you."

Of course, I could see very little through my tears of joy. But I noticed someone was missing. "Where is Sōtōko?"

They all became silent.

"Blessed Amida," whispered Papa. "Has she left this world, too?"

"Worse!" said Kiwako. "She has chosen to marry one of Lord Tsubushima's sons!"

"The blame is mine," said Mama, bowing her head. "I was so sick with worry over Amaiko and Mitsuko and what would become of us that I did not discourage the girls from socializing with Lord Tsubushima's sons."

"Sōtōko actually fell in love!" said Kiwako. "Can you believe it? She would not come out with us because she feared you would forcibly take her away from here."

Papa rubbed his chin. "If it is her will to marry, it could be advantageous to have our families joined so."

Kiwako stared at Papa, aghast, but he rode forward and shouted up at the castle walls, "Tsubushima-san! One of my daughters is missing!"

Lord Tsubushima came back to the castle wall. "The one you speak of, Munetame-sama, has chosen to remain among us, as the wife of my son Riko."

"Then this is excellent news, Tsubushima-san. What

father does not want his daughter to find a good marriage? Let her come out so that I may give proper felicitations. I assure you, I will not remove her against her will."

After conferring with his men a moment, Lord Tsubu-shima said, "You are right, Munetame-sama. Let us make this an opportunity for peace between us. Be so good as to wait a short while and we may solemnize the joining of our families this very hour."

What came to pass may have been the strangest and most wonderful Recognition of Marriage ceremony that has ever been. Goranu raised his arm and signaled the other tengu "warriors" to form a half circle at the edge of the clearing in front of the castle. The dragons in the sky churned the clouds with their tails until the last rays of the setting sun shone through and the clearing was roofed with beams of rainbows.

The castle gates opened and servants rushed out. They set up a low platform covered with straw mats. Fine silk pillows were placed on one side of the platform, thick animal skins on the other (which was disturbing to our Buddhist family, but Papa chose not to remark on it). They set up a kichō for the ladies of our family, a screen with a fine piece of Chinese brocade (which they must have stolen from somewhere) draped over it.

As we sat behind the screen upon the red silk cushions, drums sounded from within the castle and shrill notes were blown on many flutes. We peered between the panels of the screen as the castle gates opened again and Sōtōko rode out . . . actually sitting astride a horse! With her head held high and her face uncovered. Unheard of for a proper lady!

Kiwako made a noise behind her sleeves, and I saw the slightest of frowns on Amaiko's face. Mama and Papa pretended nothing was amiss. I watched Sōtōko, fascinated, though I knew I should be disapproving.

"And she's learned how to handle falcons," growled Kiwako. "And to shoot arrows from a bow. They've turned her into a barbarian!"

"Really? How amazing!" was all I could say.

"Hush!" said Mama. "They are family now. We must be respectful."

I presumed the young man on the horse beside Sōtōko was her new husband. He was sturdy and muscular and even had a beard, like his father! Not the sort of fellow admired at Court at all. I was quite prepared to hate him. But as he helped Sōtōko dismount and accompanied her to the platform, his gaze upon her was precisely that with which Yugiri had looked upon Amaiko. Therefore I could not hate him. It seemed quite unfair.

Lord Tsubushima joined them on the platform, seating himself across from Papa. Another kichō was set up and the ladies of the Lord's family were seated there, in such a way that no matter how we craned our necks, we could see nothing of them. Mama said this showed gentility on their part, though I think the noblewomen of this mountain hold did not wish to be compared badly to us.

More servants brought out the necessary three rice cakes, (I do not know if the bride and groom had spent the necessary three nights together, and it would be unthinkable to ask) and several jars of plum wine.

As Papa and Lord Tsubushima uttered their speeches full

of praise for one another, and their families, and the bride and groom, my mind wandered. I tried to imagine the bridge that was appearing now in the Land of the Ancestors at this joining of families, and what the relatives there thought of it. Would Obaa-san be happy or shocked?

The two men raised cups of wine in many toasts, and although it was customary for a new son-in-law to live in the house of his bride's family, it was decided that Riko and Sōtōko would live in our mountain lodge, repairing it and making it beautiful again.

Finally the ceremony was over. The dragons overhead swept the clouds away as they headed back to the sea, the lashing of their tails sending back distant echos of thunder, leaving only the remnants of a glorious sunset behind.

We said our good-byes to Sōtōko—I wished I could have talked to her longer. There was so much I wanted to ask her, about horses and falcons and bows. But she seemed tired, so, at last, we let her return to the castle with her new husband.

As sunset faded into twilight, the last of Tsubushima's men passed through the castle gates, shutting them against the night.

Mama turned and regarded the tengu who had sat, unmoving, through the entire ceremony. "Who are these men, that we may thank them?"

Before Papa could answer her, there came from the "warriors" a growing din of rustle and clatter. As we watched, they altered, the banners becoming great black wings, the masks becoming the heads of ravens. Even the horses became other tengu, their neighs shifting to caws of laughter. The flames on their torches went out as if extinguished by the wind. One by one, the tengu flapped their wings and rose into the sky.

"Blessed Amida!" said Mama. "What sorcery is this?"

"They are tengu," I said, "and they have been helping me and Amaiko all along." As the bird-men spiraled up into the clouds, I realized that all the tengu were leaving, not just from the castle, but from my life as well. I ran down the road after them, crying, "Goranu! Goranu!"

One shape, black against the darkening sky, spiraled down and landed before me on the road. "Well?"

"Goranu?"

"Of course I am Goranu, you silly creature."

"It is dark. I could not tell."

"So. What do you want?"

"I wanted to say thank you. And . . . good-bye."

"Ah. You are welcome. Good-bye." He bobbed a bow and turned to leave.

"Wait!"

"Yes?"

"I . . . but . . . we have done so much together. I . . . don't you . . ."

"Ah! You think you will not be seeing me again."

"Well . . ."

"That shows how little you know. You are not rid of me yet, Little Puddle. We tengu do not forget good friends. You will be seeing more of me, I assure you."

"I will?" I cannot explain how happy this made me feel. One would think it a wretched thing to want to have the company of a demon, yet it was so.

"Indeed, Little Puddle. You have given us more enter-tainment than we have had in a long while. It is nearly as much fun to surprise lofty and ambitious lords as it is monks. Your name will be legend among us for centuries to come."

"It will?"

"So beware, Little Puddle. You may never know if the kindly old man begging alms at your door is a tengu come to pay respects. Farewell, until we meet again." He leaped into the sky and flew away after the rest of them.

"Until we meet again," I whispered. I watched him until his wings became part of the shadows between the stars.

*H*OW STRANGE it feels to again be putting brush to paper on this, my Tengu Monotagari. It has been two years since I last picked it up and gazed on its pages. It must be fate that made me look into this box today, for this very day an event has occurred that justly should be added to this story.

But how to tell it? Mama would have said begin slowly. That stories are like the paths of a sublime garden, where each feature should be a delightful detail to be savored, even though it is also part of a harmonious whole. Alas, Mama has left this world, taken by a fever last winter, so I cannot ask her advice. I hope she has gone to the Land of the Ancestors . . . I know she would be happy there. I say sutras for her every day.

What a strange afternoon. It is autumn, and the wind is warm as summer. Still, I see the clouds of winter on the horizon and I fear it shall become cold very soon. Papa worries about me. He is still upset that I have chosen to become a pilgrim and not take a position at the Imperial Court. I have reminded him that girls of the finest families serve at the shrine of Ise, but he is not consoled. Amaiko writes often, pleading that I reconsider. I do not know when I will tell her that I have decided to take the tonsure soon and join an Amidist order.

But after all I had seen, how could I live within sliding,

shadowy walls, however gilded? Much better to wander from temple to shrine, seeing all the people, the mountains, the sea. I have even ridden in a boat! It made me ill, but I am determined to try it again one day.

I have sometimes wondered if I am eager to take vows in order to avoid the harsh judgment of Lord Emma-o—I have not forgotten his anger. Sometimes his demons haunt my dreams. I stay away from cemeteries. But more, I enjoy the freedom I have found in this life. I will recite the sutras and leave my next life for the future.

Through Amaiko's letters, I have learned that little Yūshō is not so little anymore. He is on a kickball team at Court and Papa is quite proud of him. Amaiko seems no longer distressed that I disobeyed her and told Papa of how Mochi and her family had sheltered me. We had lost so many servants over those troubled days, that Papa gladly hired Mochi's whole family to serve in his household. Mochi is trying to learn to write and has sent me a few of her poems. Her hand is clumsy and the poems are unrefined, but it cheers me to see them.

Kiwako never sends letters or poems to me, but I sometimes hear about her from other pilgrims. She is making quite a stir at Court and, if she is skillful, should have caused a couple of quite delicious scandals by next year.

Sōtōko has only sent two letters. (Though there may be more that have not reached me. My travels make me difficult to find, sometimes.) But from them I have learned that she more than ever loves her life in Tamba province. She has borne two sturdy sons, and still rides horses. I hope my travels take me there someday.

I have seen Dentō, for we are sometimes at the same temple. He seems no older (but, then, I do not know where he could add another wrinkle on his face). Yet he often talks about passing on, and I fear that he will leave this world before I learn the wisdom he could teach me.

And Goranu . . . well, he was right, as he always is. Somehow, he always manages to find me when he wants to. We meet away from temples, of course, though I fear that someone might notice this behavior and think me improper. He sometimes annoys monks nearby until I ask him to stop. He tells me stories of the amazing places he goes. I try to answer with my stories, and although I think my current travels somewhat tame compared to his, he always listens with rapt attention. I think sometimes he has protected me when danger was near. We are good friends. Or have been.

I met Goranu this morning at a bridge. It crossed a wide, shallow river. Tall grasses with purple blossoms covered both banks so that all one could see were the river and the bridge and the grass. Goranu was in young man form and he seemed extraordinarily sad.

"What is it, dear friend?" I asked. "What distresses you?"

He started to speak several times, but seemed at war with himself.

"We have known each other a long time," I said. "Surely you can trust me."

"Trust?" he said softly. "I trust you more than anyone, Little Puddle."

"So, then."

"That is why I fear to speak."

"I do not understand. Do you have bad news for me?"

"I . . . I don't know."

Were he not so clearly upset, I would have laughed. "I cannot know, if you do not."

He crouched on the bridge and gazed up at me. "You have grown, Little Puddle."

"Certainly, now I have."

"Please don't laugh."

"I am sorry. Go on."

He stared at the water on the river a little while. "Do you think . . . that one who studies the teachings of the Pure Path . . . will return to a better life?"

"So it is said. Yes, I believe it."

"Do you think . . . if I study the sutras . . . I might come back not a demon, but a mortal?"

I felt a tightness inside. "But if you study the sutras . . ."

"I will die. But will I come back a mortal?"

"I cannot say. I do not know enough about these things yet. But why should an immortal be thinking of other lives?"

He slowly reached up and ran a finger along the hem of my sleeve. "You are mortal."

"And I see little advantage in it."

His gaze met mine. "You are beautiful."

I felt very strange. The world seemed to turn sideways. Now it was I who could not speak.

"We have been friends so long," he went on. "Surely our fates are now entwined and we will meet again."

"Perhaps so," I said at last. "But you are immortal. You need not leave your life to see me in a new one."

"I am a tengu," he sighed. "Only a tengu. We do not . . . mortals and we can't . . . I can only be your friend."

"You have been a very good friend."

"I want to marry you."

"Ah." My feelings were like the tides at Enoshima, surging in all directions.

"I had never really spoken to a mortal girl until I met you. I didn't know what you were like. Oh, Susano-wo sings praisingly of mortal women, but everyone knows he's crazy. But you . . . you have taught me so much. Mortals see beauty where we tengu mostly see a good joke. You write poetry. I cannot. You mortals are as cruel as we, but you have warmth and love that we do not. I . . . I want you to teach me the sutras."

I knelt down beside him. "Goranu, if you begin to find the Path, it will hurt you."

He closed his eyes. "I will die."

"But why?"

"To come back as a mortal. And then find you again."

"I have put aside thoughts of marriage."

"For this life, of course. But won't you consider it for your next? You may think about me then."

I gazed at his sad, silly, long-nosed face. "What if I do not remember you in the next life?"

"Our fates are bound together, neh? We will always know that much."

"Yes." I looked out at the reeds, blown by the wind this way and that. "I do not know if I can teach you, Goranu. I do not know if I have the strength to see you harmed, even for good reasons."

Goranu bowed his head. "I understand. You have such a kind heart. At least consider it then. I will come for your answer tomorrow." He touched my face once, then stood. For a moment, it seemed he would turn into a bird and fly away. But instead he walked away, his arms wrapped around himself. I watched him go until he was hidden by the tall grasses.

The wind moans through the eaves of this ancient temple. Even though it is warm, I shiver. I look at the setting sun through the bamboo blinds and wish I could will it to stay, so there would not be tomorrow. Dear Amida, what shall I do?

I cannot write anymore. I must go and think. I would pray for a vision, yet in this I think I must be guided by my own heart. I will put this story away now . . . It is no longer a happy tale. Forgive me, whoever may read this, for my saying no more. Perhaps it is better. You may imagine that I shall make whichever choice is most pleasing to you. As for me, I must go into the sanctuary and await the dew of morning.

AUTHOR'S NOTE

*T*HE FUN OF writing a historical fantasy is in mixing the cultural details of a place and time with mythological elements. It can be hard for a reader unfamiliar with the period, however, to know just which details are based on history and which ones the author made up for the sake of the story. In this section, I'll explain some of the background I drew upon for writing *Little Sister*.

I set the story in the late Heian period of Japanese history, approximately A.D. 1100. This period is before many of the things we commonly associate with Japan appeared (no shogun, no sushi, no Kabuki drama, no Godzilla). Heian Kyō (now modern Kyoto) was the imperial capital at that time, although the political power of the Emperor was beginning to fade.

Mitsuko and her family are all fictional characters, but the Fujiwara were an actual historical clan of great social status and power, for a long time second only to the Imperial family and sometimes acting as the real power behind the throne. But even their hold on power was not secure in the late Heian period, as they faced rivalry from other noble families.

Various other groups were starting to try to grab power for themselves; lords of outlying provinces, for example (such as the fictional character Lord Tsubushima), or the powerful temples, such as the (quite real) warrior-monks of Mount Hiei. Several times during this period, there would be rebellions in the outer provinces, or the warrior-monks would come into the capital and terrorize the nobility, marching around the Imperial Palace and chastising the Emperor for impiety. Highway robbery and burning down houses (as depicted in Mitsuko's story) happened all too often.

In those days, there was extreme separation of rich from poor, women from men. The nobility of Heian Kyō thought of themselves as "The Good People," setting themselves above anyone who labored or farmed or did anything useful, and they kept themselves completely ignorant of how the non-nobility lived. Women of noble family were separated even further: living behind screens or curtains of modesty, dressing in many layers of voluminous kimonos to hide their shapes, hiding their faces behind their sleeves in public.

Their lives were filled with aesthetic pursuits: writing poetry, playing music on a form of zither called koto, choosing the colors of their kimonos to perfectly match their social rank and the season of the year, attending festivals and parties at the Imperial Palace, and, of course, endlessly gossiping about each other. Nonetheless, these cloistered women wrote much of the lasting literature of the period, and it is from their diaries and other writings that I derived much of Mitsuko's family's attitude about what is proper and how life should be.

In those days, girls married very early (sometimes as young as twelve!). A girl of Mitsuko's age and rank would be expected to enter service as a lady-in-waiting at the Imperial Court, with the intention of catching the interest of a suitably ranked nobleman. Some noble girls, however, went to serve at one of the major shrines or temples around the city (which at least allowed them to see a bit more of the outside world).

There were two religions prominent in Japanese life at this time: Shinto and Buddhism. Shinto is an "animist" faith, based on reverence of ancestors and kami, god/spirits that inhabit awe-inspiring places or persons. It is the oldest religion in Japan, and is the foundation of much of that nation's culture. Buddhism arrived in Japan in the middle of the sixth century, from India through China, and was popular among the nobility during the Heian period. Buddhism emphasized transcendence and turning away from the material world through meditation and the study of sutras, long religious poems. Although the focuses of the two faiths were very different, they coexisted peacefully and even blended to some extent. Thus, even though Mitsuko and her family are Buddhist, they recognize and accept many Shinto beliefs.

The mythological elements in *Little Sister* are drawn from both Shinto and Buddhism. Tengu, the mischievous shape-shifters of the forests, come out of Shinto folktales, as do the deities Susano-wo and Lord Emma-o, and figures such as the Dragon King of the Sea and Princess Meiyo of Mount Fuji. The concepts of reincarnation, karma, and Miroku, the Buddha Who Is Yet To Be, are out of Buddhism.

There are other folklore elements whose origin is not as clear. The Good People of Heian Kyō were quite superstitious, relying on astrology and other forms of divination to rule their lives. They believed that good and bad luck were contagious and that demons periodically moved into parts of town, forcing the nobles to change residence or go visiting others from time to time. I tried to put elements of this folklore into the story to give the flavor of their daily lives, but I am sure I could not make it as complex as their real lives must have been.

For those interested in reading more about the Heian Japanese, I recommend *The World of the Shining Prince: Court Life in Ancient Japan,* by Ivan I. Morris; *The Tale of Genji,* by Murasaki Shikibu; and *The Pillow Book of Sei Shonagon.* The last two were written by noblewomen of the period and I used them heavily in researching the background for Mitsuko and her family.

Amida: One of the names for the Buddha, the Japanese version of Amitabha (which means "Boundless Light").

bodhisattva: In Buddhism, a spiritual being who, out of compassion delays entering nirvana in order to give spiritual assistance to mortals. In some regions, they are worshiped as saints or minor deities.

-chan: A diminuitive suffix, used between members of a family or loved ones, indicating affection.

daikon: A large white radish usually harvested in winter.

daimyo: A prince or noble lord, usually with sovereignty over a particular province.

Divination Bureau: As it sounds, an office within the Imperial Palace of the Heian emperors devoted to the study of astrology and the reading of portents in order to advise the Emperor and his lords of what days are auspicious for various events and duties

Enoshima: Formerly an island, now a peninsula on the north coast of Sagami Bay, south and west of Tokyo. In folklore, it was believed there was a cave on this island that led all the way to the heart of Mount Fuji.

Enryakuji: The temple complex at the top of Mount Hiei, founded by the monk Saicho early in the Heian period. Over time, the complex grew to nearly thirty buildings.

Fuji-sama: The Sacred Mountain, Mount Fuji, located approximately seventy miles southwest of modern-day Tokyo. Followers of Shinto believe the mountain to be a deity.

Fujiwara: The most powerful and influential clan (other than that of the Emperor) throughout the Heian period. The name means "wisteria."

gosechi: Ritual dances performed, usually by daughters of noble family, in the Imperial Palace over four days in the late fall.

Heian Kyō: Modern-day Kyoto, this city was the capital of Imperial Japan from A.D. 798 to 1867, although the actual center of political power shifted from Heian Kyō to Kamakura in 1199.

Kageru: The Shinto deity who traditionally watches over the Fujiwara clan.

kami: Usually defined as god or spirit, kami is that force that produces awe. Often associated with natural features such as mountains or rivers, it also can be associated with persons, weather, buildings, etc.

Kannon: A bodhisattva (or sometimes a goddess) of mercy.

kichō: Sometimes translated as "curtain of modesty," this furnishing consists of a cloth hung on a low frame, behind which ladies of the Heian court would sit when in the company of men to whom they were not related or married.

koto: A stringed instrument, usually described as a zither. It is a box with a curved roof over which strings are stretched. It is played by plucking the strings, either with fingers or plectrum.

Lake Biwa: A large body of water to the north and east of Heian Kyō. According to legend, it can give magical powers to whatever is bathed in its waters.

Miroku (The Buddha Who Is Yet To Be): The Buddha who is supposed to arrive on earth 5,670 million years after the present Buddha has entered nirvana.

mitchoku: A particular kind of writing paper, much prized by Heian ladies.

monotagari: A written narrative, sometimes fictional, sometimes historical, or both.

Mount Hiei or Hiei-zan: Mountain to the northeast of Heian

Kyō, on which was founded a major Buddhist temple, Enryakuji. As the temple complex grew to cover the whole mountaintop, it became more common to refer to the mountain itself when indicating the temple complex.

neh: An interrogative, such as "isn't it?"

Obaa-san: Grandmother. The name automatically takes the honorific suffix -san, due to the deference traditionally given the elderly in Japanese culture.

O-Bon (also Urabon): This festival is the Feast of the Dead, in which food is set out on the family shrines, to invite the spirits of ancestors to visit. Sometimes bonfires are lit, and there are dances and processions. It is still celebrated in modern Japan, in the middle of July.

ri: Measure of distance, equivalent to 2.44 miles.

saibara: Often translated as "folk song."

sakaki: A tree sacred in Shinto belief. Sakaki are planted within every shrine area and branches of the tree are often used in rituals.

sake: An alcoholic beverage made from rice, and usually served warm.

-sama: An honorific suffix used in addressing someone of very high status (i.e., "Lord").

-san: An honorific suffix, sometimes used as "Mister," indicating respect.

Shingon: ("Pure Word") A sect of Buddhism that believed that mystery lies at the heart of the Universe. It tended to blend the beliefs of Shinto and Buddism.

Shinto: The original folk religion of Japan and the basis of much of its culture, Shinto beliefs centered around the worship of kami and ancestors.

shōji: Sliding door, usually made of wood and paper.

Shrine at Ise: A major Shinto religious center.

sutra: A long religious poem recited as a part of Buddhist worship.

tachi: A long sword, precursor of the samurai katana, except that its sharp edge is on the concave side of the curved blade.

tengu: In Japanese folklore, a shape-shifting goblin or demon who lives in the forests and mountains. Tengu are said to take the shape of birds or people with very long noses. They are masters of magic and illusion and love to harass monks.

Tōkkaido: A major road connecting the cities of eastern Japan.